Here Until *August*

Also by Josephine Rowe

A Loving, Faithful Animal

Stories

Josephine Rowe

Catapult
New York

This is a work of fiction. All of the characters, organizations, and events portrayed in this novel are either products of the author's imagination or are used fictitiously.

First published in the United States in 2019 by Catapult (catapult.co)

ISBN: 978-1-948226-07-3

Cover design by Jenny Carrow
Book design by Wah-Ming Chang

Catapult titles are distributed to the trade by Publishers Group West
Phone: 866-400-5351

Library of Congress Control Number: 2019932409

Printed in the United States of America
10 9 8 7 6 5 4 3 2 1

I know what I see; sun that could be
the August sun, returning
everything that was taken away.

LOUISE GLÜCK, “October”

Contents

Here Until *August*

Glisk

We are wading out, the five of us. I remember this. The sun an hour or two from melting into the ocean, the slick trail of its gold showing the way we will take.

Ahead of me my tiny sister sits regal and unafraid in the middle of the raft that Fynn has built of packing foam and empty chemical buckets, lids fixed airtight with caulk. He's already tested it out in our neighbors' pool and declared it sea-worthy, but if the thing falls apart he has promised to carry Sara himself. Fynn is thirteen, older than me by five years, and the only one of us three kids who has been out to the island before. Our mother had long hair then, and Fynn's dad was still around, hadn't yet skidded his motorbike underneath a roadtrain one rainy December night. My dad—Fynn's dad now too, Mum constantly reminds us—shoulders a picnic basket filled with Sara's favorites, Fynn's favorites, Mum's favorites, mine: cheese-and-apple sandwiches, salt-and-vinegar chips, slivers of mango doused with lime and chili, ginger beer. Enough food to last a week, though we'll be crossing back to the mainland this same night, lit by a quarter moon and a two-dollar torch.

The people around us hardly seem like people. More like a muster of herd animals. They move steadily through the water in ones and twos, feeling for the slope of the sandbar underfoot, the treacherous edge where the ocean floor falls away. That's how people—tourists, mostly—get themselves drowned, snatched off by rips.

The sea the sea the terrible . . .

Yep yep, we say, we know; Dad gets wordy sometimes.

There are other families, some towing small children on boogie boards, inflatable li-los, nothing so fine as Sara's raft. Coolers bob alongside clothes tied inside plastic shopping bags, silver jellyfish-balloons with Day-Glo guts.

We're lucky, Dad's telling us. Today is a neap tide—safest time to make a crossing. The highest tide not as high as normal, the deepest part not so deep.

Farther out the island looks like a rough dog slouching up from the ocean, muzzle pointed northwest. What's out there? A lot of putrid birds, Fynn's already told me, and some all right caves, mobs of bogans sinking tinnies of lager. Nothing awesome. But tonight, after sunset, the shores around the island will be aglow with the visiting swarm of bioluminescent phytoplankton, on their anxious, brilliant way to who-knows-where. We'll perch along the highest bluff in a sprawl of blankets while the waves crash iridescent against the rocks below, sweeping away to leave lonely blue stars stranded here and there, then charging back in to reclaim them.

It will be spectacular, an eerie sort of magic, and I will never see anything like it again.

But whatever, this isn't the point. In the end, the island is just a dog-shaped rock covered with birds and sunburnt gawkers, temporarily surrounded by terrified dinoflagellates.

It's this wading out that matters, this crossing: the bright, migratory-animalness of it. Going waist deep, chest deep, waist deep again. What matters is how, halfway over, Fynn looks back at us, then ahead again, and says to no one, or everyone, or maybe just to Sara:

I reckon this is how the afterlife must look.

I see Dad look at Mum and mouth the word: *afterlife?*

Fynn is the palest of us, lighter even than Mum; blond all the way to his eyelashes, the only one who crisps up in the sun. He looks adopted. A thing we all know but know better than to say.

Anyway. There it is.

Do I make it through childhood without staking every possible biological claim on the man who calls us both *my beloved savage*? I'm ashamed to say I do not. I'm content to share him only in his lesser moments: it is *my* dad who used to play bass in an almost-famous blues band, but it is *our* dad who, before the blues band, used to play clarinet in a high school orchestra. It is my dad who promises to buy us a pair of albino axolotls, our dad who reneges when Fynn and I neglect our goldfish duties and Skeletor's tank is all slime and fug.

(There was a time, some years, where it was just Fynn and Mum, and this is maybe what I'm getting back at him for. Or else I'm getting back at him for all the names he isn't called in school, the way no one ever asks where he's from, whether his parents are *reffos*. Or else it's the fact that, even though one of them is dead, he has two fathers, doesn't have to share his, and is allowed to wander off without telling anyone, to give reasons like *just thinking* or *just walking*, getting soft looks instead of strife.)

Does my brother find some spiteful way of getting even, of undermining my full-bloodedness? He never does. Maybe he never feels the need to. Fynn takes these pissing contests for what they are. In actual pissing contests, there is no competition, and really no point. He gets halfway to the bougainvillea tumbling over the top of the fence, while I try (no hands) not to dribble on my runners.

*

At the deepest point of the crossing, the ocean reaches my lower lip, and I hold on to Mum. Feel my feet levitate from the shell grit below. Become cargo swinging from her strong gold shoulder, safe in her smell of coconut oil and warm bread as she pushes on towards the island.

Around us the ocean thickens to an algaeic soup that stinks of dead things; proof that the plankton are here, though invisible for now—it isn't dark enough to give them away yet. This is the point where Fynn's raft begins to keel, the empty buckets unhitching, and Sara responds with a lot of high-pitched wailing and clutching at salty air.

When the raft breaks apart, Fynn keeps his word, and Sara scrambles up from the wreckage to ride his bony shoulders, her little grabby starfish hands clenching fistfuls of his tawny hair. It must hurt badly, his face like a cheap rubber mask of itself, but he says nothing while trying to shepherd pieces of the debris ahead of himself.

Waves slap at his face, trying to get in through his mouth and nose. He screws his eyes shut, snorts water, while higher up Sara sings, oblivious, her stubby little feet hooked under his wrists.

Hey mate, Dad offers, I can take her. But both Fynn and Sara shake their heads, so Dad just cruises alongside in a coastguardish sort of way, until the ocean finally slips from Fynn's shoulders and leaves Sara cheerily marooned up there.

There are no photographs of this day. Mum dropped the disposable QuickSnap crossing back to the mainland, and though we groped and kicked around no one turned it up. Perhaps that's why I remember it so vividly. Fynn stumbling through the breakers with Sara, delivering her safely to the dry sand and waiting until Mum had led her off to squeak into some penguin burrows before he doubled over and gushed out all that swallowed seawater into a patch of saltbrush. Fiery stinger marks striped his quaky legs.

Years later, somewhere into adulthood, I'll decide that this is a story to one day tell at my brother's wedding. Or else his funeral. Possibly both—as with a certain kind of suit, it seems workable for either occasion.

Instead of the wedding and/or funeral speech (though sure, there's still time enough for both) I'm delivering this story to my wife. Trying to wrest my brother back from what local mythology has made of him. Careless Idiot at best. Murderer at worst. Ti has been driving past those crosses at the shoulder of Highridge Road for years, since before we even met. Shed-made, white as desert-bleached bones. Coated with a fresh layer of paint every spring, strung with teddy bears, ribbons, other sentimental lark. Trinkets refreshed each September. The grandparents' work, we suspect; the father too modest for that sort of rubbish.

This is all Ti knows of my brother. This, and the couple-three cards he's sent, and the shedful of furniture he left behind; all gliding teak curves and high-tension wires. *Mid-century harpsichord*, Ti calls it, explaining how *their* father was a luthier when friends admire the coffee table, the only piece that makes sense with the rest of our house.

My father, I'll sometimes add. My father was the luthier.

Why, Ti wants to know, would your brother come back here?

I ask myself the same.

After the hearing, depending on who you care to ask, Fynn either *ran*, *slunk*, *snuck*, *crawled*, *choofed off*, *fucked off*, *hauled arse*, or simply *went* to the Northern Isles of Scotland, where the Atlantic charges in to meet the North Sea, and where he got some shit-kicking work at a whisky distillery. There he puts in five or six shifts a week, making nothing that anyone could put his name to.

I still draw sometimes, he told me once, glitchy at his end of our sole Skype attempt. His face freezing then catching up with itself.

I still sketch out ideas for things I might make one day if I ever [garble].

Last year Mum and Dad retired to Norfolk Island, from where Mum phones every Sunday to talk politics and weather and to ask what the hell she did wrong. Sara is twenty-five, working as an image and style consultant in Sydney. Who knows what she thinks; she's less scrutable than a butchy boy. She doesn't remember that trip to the island, or the raft, and I'm not sure she remembers a time when she liked either of us, Fynn or me.

Her first memories start at five, and by then Fynn was sixteen, flakey as a box of Frosties, and I was a monster. Long gone are the days when she would laugh along with whatever jokes we told, not understanding but not wanting to be left out. Sometimes we would laugh just to make her laugh, tell jokes that weren't funny, or weren't even real jokes but had the rhythm of jokes. Just to test her, to watch her go. Now she doesn't find anything funny.

I think you ruined her, Mum says down the phone one weekend. You and that brother of yours.

When did he become mine? is a question I do not ask.

Fynn arrives on a Saturday morning with one duffel bag, his blondness gone to seed, hair brushing the collar of the bomber jacket he wears in spite of the January heat. Dead pine trees still line the curb, flung out for green waste.

My brother lopes across the scorched front lawn, looking even older than he did in court, older than I figured possible. Walking taller than he wants to be, ghosting up the morning. Out on the street there's his rental hatchback, some hairdryer, crouching as though it, too, hopes not to be seen. As though six years might be too soon.

I'm waiting behind the flyscreen, feeling everything I'd neatly flat-packed springing up in me. I will punch him, I think. No, I will bring him in close. I will tell him . . . I don't know what.

Yes, I might've picked him up from the airport, traveled

that eighty K with him—school doesn't start back till February, the course is all set, no one needs a thing from me till then. But I was thinking, To hell with it. After this long and this much silence he can manage, at least, to make his own way back here.

He's turning silver gray at the temples, and when he finally looks up his blue eyes waver as though he is gazing at something unstill. He reminds me of those huskies that people, out of vanity or stupidity, see fit to keep as pets in this climate. Ti's hands ball into little fists when she sees them, these bewildered, patchy-coated animals paraded around Perth's richer suburbs, humiliated wolves.

Fynn is humiliated, of course. He is beyond humiliated.

Hey! I say. Then, like an idiot, Welcome back!

Raf, is all he says, putting his hand forward like I'm about to go and shake it.

I step out into the glare and grab him around the shoulders, and he stands there stiffly for a few seconds, finally relenting to the hug.

Still in the doorway he rummages through the duffel bag. Brought you a gift, he says, but he says it like *geft*, this new lilt in his voice. Your wedding, he says, handing over a fancy wooden booze box. Sorry I missed . . . Then he waves a hand to mean: Everything.

It strikes me that this is what strangers do. Make offerings before stepping over the threshold of each other's house. That this is what we are now.

Get in here, would you?

Inside he shucks off the bomber jacket. His skin is the bluish white of those axolotls Dad never bought us.

Six summers, he explains, like an apology. A lot to make up for—mind if I go photosynthesize? Then he spends the next few hours just lying in our backyard, stripped down to his undies. Ti will be at work a few hours yet, dislodging pieces of Lego from the throats of small stupid dogs, treating pissed-off cats for gingivitis. Fynn keeps his eyes closed as we speak about nothing much: Mum and Sara synching up their mid- and quarter-life crises; the Perth mining boom; the resulting ice boom; the inevitable rehab boom.

I rant about my students, mostly write-offs. Teaching them the difference between Rhizaria and Chromalveolata when it'd be more use teaching them the difference between papillomavirus and chlamydia.

All the while my brother's face is turned directly towards the sun. I study the frail red and gray blood vessels on his near-translucent eyelids, limpid as rock pool creatures down there in the deep set of his skull. The drive from the airport would have taken him past those crosses, the gleaming reinforced barrier.

What? he says from behind his closed eyes.

Nothing. You're burning, you know.

Beaut. Fine by me. Six bloody summers . . .

Yeah yeah.

My wife falls in love with him, of course. Not in any way that could really be considered dangerous, just in the way I knew she would, the way people have always fallen in love with Fynn; quickly and easily and faithfully. *It is so so so good to finally finally meet you*, like a record jumping, and suddenly the crosses planted at the shoulder of the highway do not stand for two tiny girls and their singing-teacher mother. They stand for small-town intolerance, grudges borne longer than is fair or necessary, nourished by the kind of rural oxygen a larger city would have starved them of.

The two of them stand at the kitchen sink, elbow to elbow, debearding mussels. Cracking up over something I don't catch. In high school the couple of girls I managed to bring home laughed just as easily for him, like they were trying to rouse some sleeping thing. Fynn, my older, whiter brother, who never felt the need to take me down a notch. Who's always had everything going for him. Why do I still think of him this way? And why is there a moment, a flash in which I also think, *skulked*, *snuck*, *hauled arse* . . . after all the defending I've done in the years between the accident and here. Especially in the first months, with people murmuring and shaking their heads in the tinned-veg aisle, though all I have in common with Fynn is some blood.

I'm watching them over the top of my beer, my brother and my wife, somehow knowing, before it happens, that one of them is going to slice the paring knife through their palm, and the other is going to have an excuse to come at them with

Dettol and cotton wool, and that I'm going to have to sit here and watch this. Then Fynn goes *Ah Christ!* but the gouge isn't deep, doesn't need Ti's attention, and he gets on with the job of scraping away the hairy tendrils that once anchored the mollusk someplace it thought sturdy.

Soon enough we're sitting around the table, butterflying shells between our fingers, using the halves for slurping up the briny liquor, the house filling with a fragrant, kelpy smell.

Ti has a theory about labor-intensive food, the kind where utensils are a waste of time and attempts at grace just make you clumsier. This theory holds: the empty shells pile up between us and the talk spills easy, as if we've been doing this every Saturday for years, the three of us.

The work's mostly just menial stuff, Fynn says. Bottling, labeling. Keeping the mice offa the malt floor. Things I can't mess up too bad. No hand in the art of it. But it's enough to be in that landscape—that old, that immense. Part of you just disappears.

All of you just disappeared, I think.

Got a little boat, he's saying. Take it out for sea trout on my days off. Bay of Isbister, Inganess . . .

When he says these names it's with that glint, as though the words have been kept in the wrappers they came in.

We drink all the wine that wasn't used to steam open the mussels, and when that's done we crack Fynn's wedding present. I uncork the heavy-based bottle, and the North Sea rushes into the room. I slosh out three glasses and we lift them to the wedding. We lift the next round to Dad's bypass, then another to the cousin whose dive gear let him down, and all the things that Fynn shouldn't have missed but did and oh well what can you do he's here now, hey?

Ti's giving me that *watch it* look. Fynn clears his throat and unfoots a mussel with a twist of fork, then goes back to seducing her with northernmost Scotland's beauty and gloom. The peat slabs cut and lifted out of the ground, snaked through with heather roots and reeking of time. The salt air and natural violence that make their way into the bottle. The ocean and how it differs, how the memory of Western Australia shrinks right down to a pinhole. Standing at the edge of the Yesnaby Cliffs, clouds of guillemots beating frantic overhead.

Like the very ends of the earth out there, Fynn says.

Like the afterlife . . . ? I edge in, and I can tell from how he looks at me that he doesn't remember ever saying that, that he thinks I'm taking the piss. None of us are quite drunk enough to not be embarrassed by this, so I refill our glasses and we drink to our sister, whose sense of humor we incrementally destroyed.

The bottle makes seven or eight rounds before it's drained, and by that stage Ti has tapped out, her sturdy brown legs drawn up beneath her on the couch, her dark hair curtaining her from our nonsense.

Without her voice to anchor us there comes a drift, a silence so big and awful that it could be holding anything, but I know what's lurking within. I try to head it off with small talk, but Fynn just nods. Here it comes, I think. Here it is.

You've seen him around, I s'pose?

Who?

Fynn shakes his head, as if I'm the coward.

Yeah. I see him sometimes. Not all that often.

And?

Look. Fynn. There's nothing I can tell you that's going to make you feel less shitful about it. Last year I saw him at the Farmers' Arms, and he looked like a man whose wife and kids had died five years ago. A few months back I saw him at the post office, and he looked like a man whose wife and kids had died six years ago. What else is there to say?

It happened in a heartbeat. In a *glisk*, Fynn has since said. Swerving to miss the dog that came trotting out of the scrub. Swinging his ute into the oncoming lane, into the oncoming sedan. Just a glisk, then. And the safety barrier just for show, apparently, eaten through by salt air and melting away like bad magic at the first kiss of fender.

I met a woman, Fynn says. Sweet clever type from the library. When I'd stay with her overnight, there'd be the sound of her kids running around the house in the morning. Sound of them laughing downstairs or talking in funny voices to the cat. It was too much, Raf. I couldn't tell her. And I couldn't stay.

I keep looking for something, my brother goes on. Something that'll fill up this scooped-out place but drink doesn't do it. Sex doesn't do it. I walk, I walk a great fucking lot, and the wind there wants to rip you open, but it isn't enough. I'll think maybe I can lose it in a roomful of people, like it'll be made to seem smaller somehow, but no, it's like everyone can all already see it, smell it on me.

I make to recharge our glasses, then remember there's nothing to recharge them with.

You want to know the best it gets? Really, the best it gets?

Come on, I tell him, get your stupid jacket.

I'm further over than he is but I know the last thing he wants is a steering wheel to hold. I climb in the driver's side of Ti's Golf, fix the mirrors while Fynn hides his eyes behind a pair of aviators.

You don't want those. Anyway, you still look like you, just more of an arsehole. Everyone looks like an arsehole in aviators.

Right, he says, flinging them into the lantana.

Since Fynn left, some Perth kids came down and reopened the Kingfisher Hotel. The smoke-damaged collection of taxidermied birds that made it through the 2009 fire—suspected arson—are still roosting about the liquor shelves. The fiber optic thing is still there, the pool table is still there. But the bar's been refitted, a big slab of reclaimed red gum, and behind it the top-tier stuff is seven tiers up, and the bartender has to put down his copy of the *DSM-5* or whatever and hop a ladder to get to it.

These boys don't know Fynn. These boys will pour him his drink without asking just how he likes being back home.

We take bar seats opposite a singed black cockatoo, its glassy eye on the rum selection. Fynn wins the wallet race, the leather split like overripe pawpaw, gaping fifties.

You need to carry all that around?

From the Travelex. I closed all my accounts when I left Australia.

You really weren't planning on coming back, huh.

Guess I wasn't.

There are Fynn's hands, threaded mangrove-like around his glass. Roughened by work that has nothing to do with him, work that carries nothing of himself. In my shed there's a second table and a set of chairs and a bookshelf. In February it heats up to a million degrees in there—*six bloody summers*—all the wood has buckled and split along the joins, the wires gone slack or snapped, all that careful tension ruined. I should have kept them in the house. I should have driven into Perth this morning, been there waiting when he hefted his bag off the luggage carousel. Now it's all I can do to lift my pint glass and meet his.

Lang may yer lum reek, Fynn says, *r*s rolling all over the place.

And may the mice never weep in your pantry, or whatever.

Close enough—where'd you turn that up, now?

Oh, y'know. I shrug and swallow beer froth. Scooped it out of the punnet.

Fynn grins down into his collar. Can ya move the Camira? I need to get the Torana out to get to the Commodore.

And the laughter that finally finds us feels very frail, but true enough, an echo rippling from the thousand family dinners spinning off lines from the same stupid shows while Mum cracked up in spite of herself, and Dad threatened to drive us out into the bush and lose us.

Of course the guy was always going to appear, company cap pulled low, eyes shaded from the glare of pool table fluorescents. It takes him a moment I see it, my brother sees it—to register that it's really Fynn sitting here, and when he does it's as if all the doors have blown open at once, the air pressure changes that fast. And if the glasses in their corral don't shatter, and the stuffed birds don't take flight . . . if the tables don't upend of their own accord, it's only because of the steadying hand someone puts on the fella's shoulder, guiding him back to the game, to his shot, to the rip of felt as he jabs too hard with the cue, the crack of the white against the five and the grinding roll in the belly of the table as the ball is captured there.

'Shot, someone says.

Fynn is already fumbling at the zip on his jacket.

Sit down, I tell him. Finish your drink.

Raf, we can't stay here.

Well, I'm finishing mine. I take a long, purposeful swallow to show him.

Fynn doesn't reach for his. Is he looking?

Christ, I'm not looking to see if he's looking.

I can't just sit here and pretend like . . . I should go say something.

What's to say? I told you, there's nothing. Just finish your drink, for fuck's sake. (When what I'd meant to say was: Brother. Be still. We're okay here.)

Fynn sits down, visibly shrinking inside the jacket's bulk.

I watch this, and I don't know what good I'm trying to force. Or even if it's good.

Right, I tell him, setting my glass beside his. You're right. Jiggety-jig.

The way home is all roadkill and future roadkill—scarpering night creatures—streaking through the high beams. Bundles of fluff and mashed feathers at the side of the road.

Acquitted, I remind him. Everyone knew it was not his intention to run three quarters of a family off a sandstone bluff. Everyone understood that. At least officially.

Okay, yes, it's awful, it's tragic, but it wasn't your fault.

How much quiet is there before Fynn clears his throat and goes, Listen. Raf? There never was any dog.

I say, How do you mean, no dog? Because I had seen the dog. Just as clearly as if I'd been riding shotgun for that nightmare. Fynn's described it a hundred times—that mongrely, greyhoundish thing, ribs on display through its sorry sack of gray skin. The way it skittered out of the scrub like a wraith. Looking over its scrawny shoulder, as though something back there had spooked it senseless.

There just wasn't. I don't . . . Can we leave it at that?

No, I think. No, we cannot leave it at that. But I drive the dark highway and keep quiet. Where had it gone then, the dog? Fynn had looked for it, in the first hundred versions of the story. He'd stood at the mangled safety barrier and dialed triple zero—that part is fact; that part is on the record—and wondered, moronically, he said, where the fucking dog had got to. *Because I wanted to kick it.* His right knee bloody and ragged from where it had been crushed up against the ignition. A BAC of 0.03. Two beers, sober enough. This is also on the record.

If not the dog?

I roll us in, silent, to the driveway. Past Fynn's rental car, which has been tipped up on its side, exposing its shiny undercarriage. We get out and stand beside it without speaking for a moment, the air full of insect and sprinkler music.

Happens all the time, I lie. It's what these kids out here tip instead of cows.

How many people would that take?

Probably doesn't weigh much more than a cow. Should we flip it back?

It only takes a halfhearted shove. The car lands with a crunch that brings about a flurry of curtain movement all up and down the street but nothing breaks and no one yells. The passenger door is scraped up and the wing mirror is cactus.

Insurance?

Fynn just breathes in long and deep through his nose.

No way it's connected, this and the blokes at the bar. They were still there when we left. Just one of those freak coincidences. I'm saying all this to Fynn and he's saying nothing.

Inside, Ti has left the couch made up with sheets and pillows, and laid the coffee table—Fynn's coffee table—with a glass of water and a pack of aspirin.

Keeper, Fynn says, with a smile so pissweak I have to tell him g'night.

Ti gives a little moan as I slide in with her, fit my knees into the backs of hers. My chest against her spine, face pushed into her hair. Her hair smells like the ocean. I slide my hand between her thighs, not really to start something, just to be there, and we stay tangled like that, drifting nearer to and farther from sleep, until headlights flood the room.

It's nearly 3 a.m. when he shows up, swaying out there on the lawn. The father, the widower. So drunk he's practically dancing, a boxer or bear.

He pounds the door fit to unhinge it, but his voice is surprisingly soft when he says, It's not right. It's not right that it's me coming to you.

No, I hear Fynn answer. I know it's not.

There's the click of the screen door as he steps onto the veranda, before I can tell him, Don't. Don't say shit. About the dog. About the complete lack of dog. He doesn't need to know. Don't say a damn word.

I drag the sheet with me into the hallway, holding it around my waist. Through the flywire I watch the two of them cross the lawn towards the street, then farther on into the night air, away from the house. Away from help. My brother wading out into the dark and the dark folding over the top of him like a wave. No right thing now, no best thing. Nothing so easy as lifting a child onto his shoulders and carrying her safely above the grabbing sea.

Real Life

It's Blind Willie McTell playing when they carry her out. "I Got to Cross the River Jordan," one of the later, elliptical versions, where he lets the guitar finish half his lines. *Nobody can . . . but Lord I got to . . . in that cold clay.* Later I'll get snagged on the morbid coincidence of this and Jody will shrug it off as nothing, point out that pretty much any blues number from his late father's collection would have seemed fitting. Maybe so. But in the moments before Madame Ayliffe's door swings open, before the paramedics shuffle onto the far end of our shared balcony and I know to feel otherwise, the McTell song seems assertive, almost joyous, and I'm happy just to be out here, bare-shouldered, tapping the scissors on my thigh to keep time.

Saturday afternoon, the sun sinking into skin like teeth into kitten-scruff. Everyone placid with it, eyes narrowed to dreamy slits. I'm out here cutting Jody's hair, Jody docile in a foldout chair with his forearms resting on the balcony railing, head tipped forward so that the snippings fall over the side and are scattered before they reach the courtyard three stories below.

Birds'll make nests of that, he says.

Not if they have any self-respect.

On the balcony beneath ours, the Yukon Jack girls. Somehow they manage to put that stuff away by the case, just the two of them. Their arguments, along with their heat, rose up through our floorboards all winter. Now they're a sprawl of legs and magazines. The Husky One and the Unhusky One. We pass them all the time on the stairs. Nodding hello like we never hear them threatening each other, or talking dirty. The ventilation broadcasts everything, indiscriminately, from the weather to sports commentaries to new slang for pussy and whore.

Jody's listening now while I cut, transfixed by what can be seen of the girls' bare feet, toes painted fluorescent orange, curled simian around their balcony rails. An outflung arm fanning a copy of *Elle Quebec*. But they only speak to each other in cool transactions. Just *Donne-moi le!* and *Bouge ta jambe!*, and the sound of ice being rummaged around inside a cooler. Nothing juicy or vocabulary boosting.

These first sleeveless days have slunk in late, a full week into May, no less, where we and everyone else have been waiting to pounce on them with dirty laundry and spritzed Aperol. When Jody rode up from Louisiana he was brown and gnarled with odd muscle he'd gained working on his uncle's bowfishing charter. There were scratches from the baby ice-box alligator still crosshatching his arms. But five months lived in artificial light have left him just as soft and harrowed-looking as the rest of us in Montreal. No one can stand to be inside today, least of all him. Everyone's out here showing their paled limbs, their unscarved throats, sunning themselves like anemic reptiles. Ash branches are flashing new shoots, gaudy as kids' jewelry. On someone's radio they're warning rain, a real spring soaker, but no one can believe that from here.

Only a fortnight ago the ice rinks were still melting. Already the slackliners have taken over, rigging up their webs all through Parc La Fontaine and wavering from tree to tree with arms outstretched. Already the work crews have been dispatched to patch up roads that fissured open during the deep freeze.

Yesterday I passed a freshly paved square of sidewalk outside the Pharmaprix. A woman had pulled up her stroller and was pressing her baby's bare feet into the wet cement. Holding him under the arms and sort of dabbing him into the gray paste, while he shrieked in glee, though it was then only 12 degrees in the sun.

Put some shoes on that kid, I almost said but didn't. I suppose some small, still unbitter part of me recognized that most of us have to take posterity where we can get it.

*

This apartment is an old one, its radiators mummified under several decades of paint, murmuring like pigeons or clanking like geese, depending on the hour. Marie, my former roommate, took all the curtains with her, and the living room became a big glowing terrarium for anyone who cared to look up from the street. Some of her things still haunt the rooms; enough to sleep on, sit in, cook with, drink from. There's a recipe for banana crepes in her handwriting, taped inside one of the kitchen cupboard doors, and the bathroom cabinet still smells faintly of her vitamin C. The lease is good until Canada Day, which Montreal reassigns as Moving Day and celebrates by hauling furniture up and down treacherous external stairwells in drenching heat. When July rolls around I can either sell this stuff on to the next tenants, or post it online, or I can chop it all down into matchsticks and toss them into the alleyway: Marie said she really couldn't give a shit.

It wasn't anything personal. As the city shook its fiery coat of leaves a dread had crept into Marie's heart, curled up snug, and refused to budge. Midway through October she dropped out of Life Sciences and then out of Quebec.

Marie believed she was blessed, and who knows, maybe she was. As a parting gift she blessed me a thumbprint-sized piece of scallop shell and told me it would lead me to providence.

I carried it around in my coat pocket the rest of fall and into winter, worrying at it until all the ridges had worn down and it was fingernail-smooth. How many years of ocean, of tumbling waves would that have taken? I felt mighty as the sea, having worn it down like that with only my nervous energy. *Now what?* I would've asked Marie, but by then she had moved back to Renfrew. I was alone with the sound of the radiator and other lives coughing through the walls.

Now and then my mother called from not-even-Oshawa, sounding more and more, to my sharpening ear, like a complete hoser. This appraisal treacherously failed to acknowledge her raising me on Anne Carson and Japanese stoneware and black lava salt, tastes that could only just be sustained with a single, part-time income in public health. She had looked into a lot of hideous mouths to see me through McGill, as she was so fond of reminding me. I'd taken a gap year in Mexico, followed by a second gap year nurturing an acquired taste for eighties telenovelas, and finally my mother said that if I didn't use the tuition money to learn something she was going to take her girlfriend to see the Panama Canal.

But I, too, dropped out of university, out of Life Sciences. In a misjudged effort at gratitude, I held out until mid-November: two weeks past the refund deadline. Making a farewell round of the preserved sea creatures and fetuses lined up in jars, their eyes and nostrils still sealed, I decided not to tell my mother, not yet. (I could pay her back, I promised her, inwardly. She would escape to Panama, after all.) I stayed on in the city, picking up a job folding towels and refreshing rooms at a fancy day spa I could never have afforded to visit. It was the best I could do, and maybe a little better than I could do. I might have fared all right in France, but I barely had enough French to be a waitress here.

The job meant waking at 6:45 every weekday. The apartment next door would already be lit up with French radio. Proof of life over there, behind the complex alarm system that seemed excessive and out of place in our semi-decrepit graystone. *Just what are they fortifying?* I wondered. *Meth lab. Snuff set. Storehouse for rare smuggled reptiles.* But as far as I could tell the sole occupant was a flossy old thing who rarely left her apartment. We shared a balcony, though, and once or twice I'd seen her out there, wind lifting her hair to show a high forehead of dark-veined porcelain, the exiled contessa of some vanished nation. The first time we exchanged words, she'd shuffled out wearing only a quilted paisley housecoat to glare towards the mountain. Nearly all of the leaves had fallen from the trees, and now the view was clear to the lurid cross.

T'es encore là? She spoke to the cross, not to me. To me she said, *Il te faut un casque*, and knocked on her fragile head.

Marie had taken her helmet but left her bicycle, and each morning I carried it downstairs and clattered it over the fissured streets towards the day spa on a route that still took me past Leonard Cohen's house. If my mother called I'd make a point of telling her this, that every morning I rode past Leonard Cohen's house, evidence that I was still studying.

I spent the first weeks of winter alone, wandering the apartment's half-empty rooms. Its windows are the old sash kind that mean trouble in the winter, but in the kitchen there are panels of colored glass that shoot red and amber oblongs across the floor when the sun finds the sweetest angle, so it feels kind of warm even when it isn't. One morning I stood there, moving my hand through red light to gold, thinking: This is the kind of window where if you just stand for long enough, somebody will come and put their hand on your shoulder. Whoever it is you've been waiting for. Then my phone rang, and my heart kicked, but it was only an automated female voice congratulating me on a free trip to the Bahamas. I listened to the spiel of promises, thinking how someone had gone into a studio and recorded these words, understanding how they'd be used. And someone had written the script, and someone had mixed the levels, and someone else . . . on and on. It made me bone-sad, this voice. I hung up on it and called Jody to ask how he was spending the off-season. There was no off-season, he said. But after five months of guiding tourists through the backwaters of Plaquemines Parish to shoot at floodlit gar, of tossing marshmallows at tame alligators to distract whiny tourist children, he'd about had it with Louisiana anyway.

I tried to sell him winter. It took less than fifteen minutes to sell him winter. He'd never lived a real one, a northern one. Never owned a pair of ice skates or salted a driveway.

Cheap post-rock concerts, I coaxed. Nuit Blanche. Poutine (this felt like groveling). The pastéis de nata at the Jean-Talon market . . .

Okay okay okay.

I should have been the one hawking Bahamas cruises.

Jody mooched a series of Amtraks up at the end of December, with $600 U.S. and no true winter coat. I snuck a look at his arms when he put them around me at Central, deep in the belly of the overheated station. A little bothered inside the elbows. Aside from the gator, I mean. Not clean, exactly, but clean enough. (*Newly clean*. Was there ever a phrase cobbled from more idiot-hope?)

Memory had slightened him. It wasn't till I saw the two of us reflected in a drugstore window that I realized how much taller he was than me. I decided to take this as further evidence of an overall straightening out.

He said that this winter's work would be liquidating his dead father's blues collection, he and his sister sharing the take.

We're selling them off piece by piece. Slower that way but you get more in the long run, according to Cass. Said she'll wire my share every couple of weeks. Less administration.

Administration, I said.

Her very precious time. One of us is our dad's child.

Wouldn't you two be, you know, sentimental? I asked. Though I knew he would not be. I'd first met him in a roachy hostel kitchen in Tamaulipas, OxyContined to his eyeteeth, making everybody sandwiches whether they wanted them or not. (You, he'd said, shaking a salsa picante bottle at me. You're avocado and hot sauce.) Afterwards he'd told me about the meds racket he and a friend were trying to get off the ground. Those were the words he used: *get off the ground.* Ailing elderly Americans with prescriptions to fill. And he objected to the term *racket*, insisting it would be a civic service. Basically an NGO. He'd be addressing a gross deficit in the health-care system, assisting those who'd slipped down into its many yawning chasms. All you needed were a minibus and the right attitude, a wholesome-looking girl. (That was me: wholesome-looking. An invitation of sorts.) He existed in a constant state of somnambulism, a soothing lassitude, but now and again you'd catch the sharp glint of scheme in his pyrite-flecked eyes.

Look, he was saying now. Dad was Mr. Corporate Law. Guy wore a suit to the beach. Wouldn't have known Blind Lemon from Blind Melon, he just knew what things were worth.

The records had been crated up in storage for eight years, and as Jody put it, someone might as well be spinning some joy from them.

I admit I was skeptical. But every fortnight we've been charging glasses to Elzadie Robinson and T. Bone Walker; rare red wax and Parchman Farm; Ed Bell and his 1930 pressing of "Carry It Right Back Home."

Someone had taught Jody the nines thing, since the last time we'd slept together. I'd read about it before, tantric: *shallow shallow shallow shallow shallow shallow shallow shallow deep*, so she—so *I*—could go along with him. He never lost count, must have gotten in a fair amount of practice. I didn't really mind thinking of that. Whoever she might've been, she was far away, too far to be jealous of, practically imaginary. It was my name he'd shout, unfailingly, in the instant before coming. Typically American of him, I said. More than any other national. Americans all call your name out—it's like they're trying to stop you walking into traffic.

Jody was nonplussed by this. Maybe hurt. Hard to tell.

It's just common courtesy, he said.

Often his orgasm would carry within it the dark kernel of a migraine. Jody would pop two acetaminophen straight after to be safe, and a couple of something else for good measure. Partaking? he'd ask, and I would, and we'd drift off together, a tangled raft of random beach junk. He'd rouse when the girls downstairs were at it again. Waking me with a little shove, Hey, what's that? What's she saying?

A game he called Fucking or Fighting? I'd listen a minute and then translate as best as I could: One of them wants to get a dog, I think, or: The Husky One thinks the Unhusky One has slept with somebody else.

The Husky One and the Unhusky One. We'd hear them all the time, but their names remained a mystery. Possibly they knew mine, with Jody so courteously hollering it.

That last one, he'd ask. What's that mean?

Mille-feuille? It's a kind of pastry, but the way she's saying it probably just means pussy. But a bit sweeter than pussy. I mean, nicer than. Ah. You know what I mean.

He did not laugh. He took it all very seriously. Repeating in that methadone drawl of his, *milfoy*, *milfoil*, *millfoey*. French by tenement osmosis.

Five days out of seven I was still getting up early to go and fold towels into pleasing shapes and wonder about the kind of women—mostly women—who would unfurl and ruin them without a blink. Men came too, but not many or often, and I didn't fall to measuring my life against theirs in the way I did with women. Especially the women my age, the ones I encountered mostly in the things they left behind: La Prairie hand creams, lipsticks in obnoxious forty-dollar shades, designer underwear, magazines commodifying mindfulness and self-love.

There was a lost-and-found, of course, but usually I either pocketed things or simply unfound them into the trash with disgust.

As winter deepened it seemed crueler and crueler to sacrifice the meager quota of daily sunlight in the service of these women.

On those night-dark mornings, the radio of our next-door neighbor was a kind of static rope I'd use to drag myself from bed, from Jody, to the kitchen. From there I hoped inertia might do the rest. The radio was loud and clear; I suppose it traveled through the plumbing, sink to sink, like the tin-can telephones we used to make when we were kids. I toasted bagels to a patter of rapid-fire Quebecois; a man's voice and then a woman's. Topical talkback. Something about the Charter of Values, military suicides. The weather report: *neige neige neige, le vortex polaire.* I was okay in high school. I got prizes in French. Now, when I tried to speak it, the words would fall out of my mouth like clumps of half-chewed bread. There was better luck listening: the words, more and more of them, floating back up towards their meanings like free divers' balloons and then hanging there, swollen and luminous. *Turnstile. Shooting. Embezzlement.*

I'd roll these words dumbly around my mouth, waiting for the coffee to brew, staring out into the dark street to see how much snow had fallen overnight. Marie's bike was useless now, chained to a railing, squirrel amusement.

Afternoons I'd come home to find Jody compulsively refreshing a web page, following the frenzied final moments of bidding as though it were an NBA playoff game he'd placed big money on. I'd empty my coat pockets of tips and tiny soaps and miniature bottles of rich body lotion, then walk around turning all the thermostats down by five degrees.

If you're cold, I'd say, why don't you put on a fucking sweater?

If you hate your job, he'd say, why don't you fucking quit?

I glanced over his shoulder. On screen, Ramblingmike73 was winning Memphis Minnie at $392, and there were still ten minutes of scrummage left.

I got us, Jody said.

But I was uncertain whether I wanted to be got. In the bathroom I arranged the gleanings from my shift into the medicine cabinet, where a few of Jody's toiletries were neatly lined up along the top shelf. Mostly this was comforting. A cottonwool-swaddled thought: How sinister a spoon looks, lying all alone on a windowsill.

Early one morning, as though a dream had leaked down into Rue Cartier: an old man, dressed in peacock green, gliding across the pond-chain of streetlights. Past the soft mounds of cars, long before any traffic came to churn up the night's pure drift.

Jody saw this, not me. I just heard about it. He'd caught sight of it from our terrarium window when he got out of bed for a glass of water. That same afternoon he went out and found a flea market on St. Laurent and came back with a pair of cross-country skis.

You can ski?

We'll find out.

Jody had never skied in his life, but neither of us doubted he'd have a knack for it. He picked up a lot of things with a striking nonchalance, drawing on a latent grace he never promised to any particular pursuit with any seriousness. Or maybe it's agility I'm talking about, not grace. He still ate like a drug fiend. Indiscriminate combinations of overprocessed, microwaveable god-knows-what. A tendency to knife-lick. *Didn't your mother ever* . . . But I could watch him move across a dark room forever.

I championed the skis. I mapped out the trails around the mountain. It wasn't as generous as wanting him to be happy;

I wanted him to not be sorry that he had come. He felt asleep here, he'd said. Dimmed and dense-souled, like on dirty horse tranqs, more ketted than benzoed.

You know you burn up just as much energy treading water as you do swimming towards something?

This was information, not a question. I've since looked it up and I know for a fact it isn't a fact, generally speaking. But it was true enough for Jody.

He said he felt dried out, alligatored by the heating system, left an apple out on the sill to show just how he meant. We watched it shrivel and leather to become a grotesque little face. Accusing.

Late into January, throwing up became my new morning ritual. In the kitchen, quietly so as not to wake Jody. The steel belly of the sink was like an amphitheater, and from within it I listened to the ghost broadcasts from next door.

. . . a confirmé plus que mille planètes extrasolaires . . .

Providence. Marie had promised. This wasn't it. Or it depended on your definition of providence. The blessed piece of scallop shell had long disappeared by then; I turned out all of my pockets but it never tumbled out.

I don't know how she knew. I didn't even *know* know; I was still hoping I was suffering from some kind of virus. But she knew. She saw me out her kitchen window one morning before work, on the balcony, inviting icy air onto my damp face, and she came out still wearing floral dish-washing gloves carrying a thermos, workman's style. Once her husband's, I figured. It was roughed up with the scratches and dents of a day laborer, or a fisherman.

English is better for you? Maybe you cannot keep anything in your stomach, but this you will manage. I know; often I can manage nothing else myself.

I wasn't showing, it was much too soon. Even if I had been, there was so much winter goosedown to disguise it. She'd heard me, then, through our little two-way sink system? Or she could tell just by looking. Maybe you gained that power of insight after seven or eight decades in the world. Maybe life knows life, I thought, feverishly sentimental.

You like it, you just say and I will bring more, she said, placing the thermos in my hands. *AYLIFFE* in faded black marker down the side.

You knock here, like so, Madame Ayliffe said, rapping at her own kitchen window, startling a small tuxedo cat off the inside sill.

At the metro station I unscrewed the lid and sniffed. It was a kind of hot ginger broth, something lemony and spicy and just a little bit sweet. I drank a dozen tiny sips, standing right there on the platform, and my stomach quietened. I finished it off in a corner of the tiny fluoro-lit staff room on my break, and felt replenished and clear-sighted, as though an ounce of grit had been sluiced from behind my eyes.

That same afternoon I was fired for turning in a wonky

swan. Really it wasn't so much the wonky swan as my "shitty attitude" about the wonky swan, about the towels in general. My general carelessness. The wonky swan was just one example. I had little grounds to argue. I finished out the afternoon, resisting the temptation of petty vengeances; mixing up the hand soaps and hair products, folding towels to resemble labia.

Jody congratulated me when I told him, as though my leaving had been a matter of integrity, my personal choice. He insisted on cooking a celebratory dinner. Something had flicked on in him, and though I knew I wouldn't keep the meal down, I couldn't refuse. All he really knew how to cook was fish, he said, promising that when spring came and we could crack the windows and doors, he'd blow the roof off with scampi, jambalaya, gumbo, things that wanted all-day bubbling to stickiness on the stove, reeking up the kitchen. But for now he was keeping it fresh and simple: kingfish puffing steam from a little tinfoil papoose; kipflers and some kind of greens on the side.

I chewed slow and careful. During a long silence, I nodded at the skis. Nobody's going to want those when spring comes, I warned him once I'd managed to swallow. You're not going to be able to resell them. You should at least try them out.

I'm going to.

You'll need to get all the other truck, I told him.

Yup.

Poles and boots. Proper gloves. All that lark.

Truck, he echoed. Lark. Do you speak that way in real life?

This isn't real life? I asked. Then I realized that if one of us didn't think so, it probably wasn't.

Maybe I'll take them back with me.

What can you do with skis in Louisiana? I tried to sound indifferent, but a slatey, astringent saliva had flooded my mouth. The something-or-other glands, I'd learned in those first weeks of class.

I forced a forkful of the kingfish and another of potato, but the acid in my mouth slurred the flavors of everything, and the textures became repulsive. I gagged, tried to swallow, gagged again, spat into a slice of bread and wadded it up like a napkin. Jody was staring at me.

So many bones, I explained. Like a little pincushion. One stabbed the inside of my cheek, I said, scraping my chair back from the old drafting board we used as a table.

Bones? he asked, prying apart the flakes of his own fish with a knife and fork. Sorry, I thought I got them all. His voice trailed me down the hallway.

In the bathroom I ran water and threw up properly. I rummaged through a drawer, hunting out a mini hotel sewing kit. The jab to the inside of my cheek felt like the first prick of a dental injection. Crazy. Did I think he'd ask to see evidence?

Fucking or Fighting? he asked when I came back to the kitchen.

What? I tongued the tender inside of my cheek.

He pointed his fork at the floorboards, cocked his head. His hair hung with the sad luster of velour. The yelps of the girls downstairs floated up.

Fucking, I answered, but didn't bother translating the specifics.

What was real life, then? It was out there, Jody's version of it. Baling wire and a worthy ache in the arms. Kicking animal feed off the bed of a Hilux, or the swamp seeping into your socks, if you were stupid enough to wear socks. His soles like burred wood, sassafras bark.

Why couldn't I tell him? Because I was a coward; if I told him, he'd decide on something. A direction, he'd pick a direction. But I didn't know which direction that would be, and I didn't trust myself not to follow it.

I slept late, woke to strong light, felt stronger myself. I filled the Ayliffe thermos with tea and took it on a walk up Mont Royal. Cross-country skiers slid past, as if on greased rails. When I reached the cross I sat for a while, looking back towards the Plateau for our apartment, but the view didn't work that way. I took a few mouthfuls of the tea, still hot and oversweet. I had come here to think, but fell into a false, wordless calm, opening the thermos now and then to let the steam breathe up into my face. But I forgot it on the bus coming home. My general carelessness, my carelessness in general. *Pas bien fait, pas bien fait.* The swan, the thermos, this other thing.

Winter lingered impossibly, and still we managed to squander it. I had thick Russian classics and some design software to master. I thought if I could just get into the kind of work that let me live out of a laptop . . . I got twenty-eight pages into *War and Peace*, and the software never made it as far as an upload. Jody's skis stayed vertical. There was talk of what to do once the roads thawed, working holidays we could take. In whose car? A bus, then, a train. Apples in the Okanagan? Apples was fall. Oranges, then. Or what comes first—asparagus? Jody looked disgusted. Down south it was strawberries.

Anyway, we never got away, winter held us close. We drank. We fucked. We downloaded old disaster movies from our childhoods and skipped straight to the quake, the volcano, the aftermath.

Coming back from the SAQ one Sunday we met Madame Ayliffe taking on the outside world. Reaching her little lavender-gloved paw out to be guided down the last few ice-glazed steps at the front of our building, where snow had obliterated the hessian grip our landlord cheapskated in place of rubber. Jody passed me the rye and ran up ahead, crooked his arm into a wing for Madame to hold on to. He led her down step for step, all southern charm, delivering her to where the sidewalk was freshly gritty with rat-bait-green salt. She grazed me with eyes blank as coat buttons, in that moment possessing no special knowledge about me, perhaps not knowing me at all. Unconcerned by thermoses, missing or otherwise. To Jody she gave no thanks in any language, just nodded her tiny marzipan head and tottered down towards the avenue. We watched after her a while, to make sure she remained upright. Her solid black shoes planted definite as small hooves.

By then I'd taken up Jody's schedule, waking at ten or later, the sun already sliding through that colored glass. Hours too late for Kitchen Sink radio, though there would be other noises from Madame Ayliffe's side of our shared wall, dish clatter or running water, sometimes wailing. I was alarmed at first, until I placed it: Cats. Cats in heat, whose yowlings always sound like maniacs doing bad impersonations of cats. Now and then a scrawny tabby appeared on Ayliffe's windowsill, twitching its tail, ears flattened. I imagined the other cats huddled in a coven, at the apartment's heart, gently rising and falling as one heap of multicolored fur.

Spring crept up on us. Bird noise then insect noise then cheers from the bars on Mont Royal as the Habs beat the Bruins in the second overtime. Stray cats lounging on stoops like sleazy little drunks. Sticky fiddleheads nudging up through the earth, unfurling to bright fronds within seconds.

Now: everything's moving, everywhere you look. Squirrels rippling up telephone poles, laundry being cranked along antiquated pulley systems, someone flapping out a bright string hammock and anchoring it between railings. Down in the alleyway, winter's hockey nets have been repurposed as soccer nets, and kids run back and forth between them, screaming a sweet patois. A woman in the building across from us is drying a load of dishes, bringing each cup, plate, bowl, fork to her back door and standing there half drunk with photosynthesis, rubbing meditatively with a nubby yellow tea towel.

I finish with Jody's hair. There you go, I tell him, spring

coat. Ruffling my hands through what's left of the shaggy brindle. It isn't a great job, but if I go any further I'll just make it worse. He won't care anyway. Or if he does, he won't say so. Released, he bounds inside for beers, comes back with them already popped and sweating.

We're just going to look at them a moment, he says, gone all reverent, laying them just out of reach. We're just going to take a minute to appreciate that it's really finally beer weather. Then he slides his icy fingers slow over my wrist, slow up to the inside of my elbow. Simple; like he's undone a zipper. I could push him right off the balcony. But there are the voices next door, and I take my arm back, wanting to see her emerge: this woman whose radio I've stopped waking with. Her balcony door opens a crack and I wait for her to shuffle out, mentally polishing a few phrases I might use, witty responses to remarks about the weather—*L'hiver ne nous a pas tué!*

From our kitchen McTell begins singing tinnily through laptop speakers, of cold wide waters and lonesome journeys, and it makes a strange matinee of the whole operation.

They must've come through the front. We would have noticed them going in, otherwise. We guess it's discretion they're trying for now, discretion that has moved them to brave the spindly swizzle stick of the fire escape, instead of the straight-up-and-down of the front stairs. A couple of days ago, even yesterday, they might have gotten her out quietly, with no one but the stray cats to flick their ears at them. But now they have a whole amphitheater of us, gawking. That woman with the dishtowel holding it at limp half-mast. Down in the laneway the kids have stopped their game, are all shining the little moons of their faces up this way. By some kid instinct they know something's up, and that it must be something wonderful, because a few of their parents are already trying and failing at calling them in.

The bag that is holding Madame lies on a stretcher borne by a stocky man and a tall thin woman, whose trouble is kept hidden under a thick ledge of bangs. They must be work, those bangs. A lot of heat and product. An effort that seems both noble and impractical given her profession.

I'm expecting the hand with its lavender glove, or perhaps a tuft of snowy hair, to be peeking out of the bag they've folded her into. Some confirmation that it's *her* in there. But she's zipped up tight, barely causing a crinkle in the stiff plastic strapped hard to the stretcher.

They have her tilted at a ridiculous angle. It won't work; she's going to slide right out, feet first, go barreling down that staircase like a sled in a luge run. The neighboring balconies have all turned opera boxes, everybody's hands over everybody's mouths, as the paramedics reverse back up the stairs. They're giving up, we think. But no, they swing around, swap places. They try at a different tilt. Headfirst, I guess, with the tall woman backing down gingerly, iron railings under her thin rubber soles. When they finally get the stretcher to ground level, someone gives three short claps that ricochet around the courtyards. Someone else joins in. An awkward, open-mic-night smatter. The stocky man looks up, smiling sheepish as though he really might bow. The woman just shakes her head.

The bangs don't move, sprayed solid. The kids do what we all want to, trailing them out to the street to watch the stretcher being packed into the ambulance.

How long?

I'm thinking of the runtish apple Jody left to wither, his experiment to show just how the heating leaches the moisture from everything. I get a flash of gums shrinking away from teeth, taste iron, push the image away.

It's only a few minutes later that the landlord emerges with a bulky orange tough bag. Sagging with cats—at least four or five of them, judging from the bulging sides of the bag, where you can see the knobby arcs of several spines showing though. And we realize: that long. It had let up weeks ago, all the yowling.

The cats, like herself, are spirited away down the fire escape. We think the landlord might dump them in the garden to deal with later, but he swings the bag right into the back of his black BMW and drives them away, as if they are evidence of violent crime. We pull on our beers, watching him round the corner. All that time she just lay in there—did she just *lie* there? And the cats, did they . . . ? I close my hand tight around a railing, my stomach pitching. Her kitchen window shows only clean white countertops, crockery stacked neatly on the draining board, a desiccated maidenhair fern on the sill.

The ambulance pulls away, sans sirens. We stay outside another couple of hours, watching the kids carry each other up and down the fire escapes. Taking turns at being swung by their hands and feet, taking turns at being dead. Dead is the most coveted role. There are accidents, of course. More than one body is dropped, and forgetting it is a body, cries out. Nothing serious. I take one more swallow of beer, but it isn't sitting right, and I let Jody have the rest.

He accepts the bottle, attention still on the kids going through their rescue and recovery maneuvers. After a moment he brushes the back of his hand against my belly, where my shirt no longer hides the swell.

He says, It'll be easy, you know.

What will?

It's just winter gain, he says, still not looking at me. It'll drop off without you even trying.

When I find no good way to answer, he takes a swig, embarrassed.

Not that you're not, you know, carrying it nicely, he assures me. What I mean is, you don't have to go depriving yourself.

I manage a nod, and he nods and knocks back the dregs.

A parent calls down from a third-floor window to shame the children for their disrespect, and they mug convincingly hangdog for at least a few minutes, before resuming their game.

At five o'clock the pressure crashes, and the storm the radio promised boils towards us so fast it's as if we are rushing to meet it, standing at the bow of a great ship. Banks of cloud like a mountain range rearing up to engulf the sky, blotting the light as in an eclipse. Leaf litter confettiing the air before the rain stamps it down in warm silver violence. The kids run circles around their yards, whooping and yelping, crazy as rain dogs.

We go inside and turn all the lights on. Then we turn them

off again and just lie down to listen. It rains us right into sleep, and when I wake hours later in the morning dark, it is still raining. Outside, the yellow haze of the city's light is spread through the wet air like mustard gas, and I can see from the shape of Jody's hair across the pillow how bad I've botched the cut. I'll offer to try again, to fix it, it will seem excruciatingly important that I fix it. But he'll say no, it's no thing. He won't get it. He's what you'd call easy. They all are, these people you can have but not keep.

In another room his laptop is still looping those five-hundred-dollar songs. McTell singing us down to hurricane season. Aluminum and wax. Fried food and petrichor. That's what it sounds like. Creosote and damp, rotting wood. Things I want but will not ask for. I get up, shut the laptop off so there's just the rain, and the radiators; the sound of doves and applause, like a magic show without the *ahhhh*.

A few more weeks and the air here will fill with down from the poplars, tiny seeds riding in airships of white fluff. A different kind of snow. My lungs filling like wet goose-feather pillows as the swallows carry mud up to the eaves for nests. Homes built with pellets of mud and grass and shit and fur—that's what's holding everything together. That's what's holding everything together. I will watch this alone, shadows of the skis against the walls.

In the kitchen I stand at the sink. I lean in, lower my head right into the stainless-steel basin, where everything is amplified. Feel the blood roll to my skull. Listen. For providence, or anything.

Nothing, nothing.

Just this warm, oceanic drift where language once was. Fathomless. I think of nostrils sealed over, eyelids near-translucent. Treading water: I was, I have been, but that's done with. Here's my foot brushing something slick and muscular, down there in the dark. I kick. We both kick.

Anything Remarkable

Certain days: it is easy to imagine this small, once-prosperous river town (barely distinct from many other small, once-prosperous river towns) as if you are only passing through it, shunpiking the thruways in favor of the scenic rural two-lanes on a road trip in your better, your best life. The life in which your formidable boxer-turned-human-rights-lawyer wife has simply pointed to this town on a much misfolded map and declared: Here, lunch. Possibly because of the town's suggestive name, possibly because she is exactly twenty-eight miles from ravenous. You promise that after this town, from this town on, you will take over your share of the driving. Neither of you slept well last night, in a three-star last-minute in the town of Lake Whoever, but you've racked up several hours of passenger-side napping while your wife listened to the final chapters of Springsteen reading Springsteen, somehow keeping the rental car out of the loosestrife.

Neither of you will have hoped for much from this town—sandwich, tank of fuel, leg stretch in view of water—so it is quick to outstrip expectation, quick to disarm you with sleek geometric shop-window typography and skeins of wild geese overhead (the geese, too, only passing through), with the ratios of porch swings to porches and tire swings to maples. The egalitarian yacht club with its yard of bright vessels (none of them yachts) wintered tight under blue-and-white ship wrap. The wood across the river a gentle riot of autumn leaves, the tree line a long, fire-feathered serpent outstretched along the bank, light breeze riffling its plumage.

There is the occasional household stars-and-stripes, draped above doorways, between Neoclassical columns, but you don't spy a single political sticker. In the spirit of cautious bipartisanship, one of you pronounces the town adorable, and the other agrees, True.

Your wife parks beside the river. She has been your wife—you have been wives—for thirteen days, since a registry ceremony on the Ontario side of Niagara Falls, planned and paid for ten months in advance, because who could be fucked waiting for Australia to get its shit together? Since there and here you've compiled a mental list of *f*s that pluralise to *v*—*life* to *lives*, *wolf* to *wolves*, *knife* to *knives*—they all sound vital and gleaming. The river has been company since Tahawus, where it traveled under a different name. But it is freshly beautiful here, at this hour, in the cold gold ameliorating light that follows rough weather.

As for the diner, it is patently ex-Brooklyn, and the menu is ex-Brooklyn, but the prices are ex-ex-Brooklyn. You order a vegetarian omelette, like a recuperating Alice Munro character. Your wife orders a turkey club that she will tear the crusts from like a child. And a quad Americano for the road (really for you).

Okay? you ask, and she answers by taking a dessert spoon from the cutlery cradle and pressing its cold contours against one heavy eyelid, then the other. She lays the spoon on the Formica table and gets up without a word to look for the toilets.

Is she still angry? Are you? Daybreak this morning, watching your wife's face, too far from your face in the mealy motel light, recataloging and reapportioning all its trouble: the superior crease near-center of her brow, last night's color stained into the deep grain of her lips. The thin, aquiline nose, twice broken; only once in the ring, only once by a woman. Your beautifully fierce, fiercely beautiful wife—what wouldn't you do for her? You're asking this now, in the ex-Brooklyn diner, asking it of the galactic melamine depths of the tabletop, fingertips seeking out the reassuring chips and divots in its surface. The server reappears with the coffee, in what looks like a soup container.

Your friend, she begins—not blinking when you correct her; *my wife*—your wife, know if she'd prefer wholewheat, rye, sourdough, seven-grain . . . ?

Rye, you tell her with nascent authority, the deceased-estate-auction ring a ratifying weight on your finger.

Your wife returns as the plates come down, heavy with home fries. You invite her into the game of wives-knives-wolves, and she ruins it.

Rooves, she offers distractedly, tearing crusts away from her sandwich. Hooves. Loaves.

The game is dead. She is still salty.

Do you want a lover or a sparring partner? you asked her early on. You ask her again now.

Both, she would have once answered. Today she says, I just want a good wife.

Wifedom is new, but the arguments feel ancient. Inherited and irresolvable. Really there is only ever the one argument, for which the American hotel has provided optimal conditions. Every room seems purpose-lit. Recalling voyeuristic large-format photographs of intimate discontent, you close the blinds. It makes little difference. The sense of audience remains.

It is not, has never been a question of Child vs. No Child. Only the interminable question of whose ovum, whose womb, whose body and vocabulary will be significantly reproportioned, whose career will take the harder spill.

Is it marriage or the American hotel room that has thrown fuel at this argument? Possibly it has something to do with the ecliptic, all-consuming silences that enfold hotel-room rows, which you've come to suspect have something to do with the size of the mattresses. Could you pass all night in your own bed, in your own home, without speaking? Your own bed is simply not wide enough. How to resist, even when righteously furious, the warm skin of your lover? At home, atop your reasonably sized mattress, it might take as little as a sole of a foot pressed to the sole of a foot, as good as *sorry*, for the blame to be made deliquescent, divisible.

The American obsession with vast mattresses—California King, Texas King—how to repair over such an expanse? It must have some bearing on the divorce rates in this country. You've cracked it. You'll write about it, for a Pacific magazine: the threat to intimacy posed by ostentatious furnishings, the correlation between acrimony and massive beds.

Crushed into your coat pocket are some erratic notes written on hotel stationery, scratched out by clock-radio light at 4 a.m., while your wife was on the other side of a memory-foam tundra. She feels nearly as far away now, on the other side of the table, refusing your eye. Perhaps still upset, perhaps simply exhausted, hungry. Her orphaned crusts are piled into a kind of brush-fence. She has never been one to talk through a mouthful.

In the hotel, you'd allowed her the last word. Or, from her perspective, had abandoned her with it, allowed it to poison the already voluminous silence:

It's not like you're currently using your body for anything remarkable.

Your body. Well. You use it to run around in sometimes. It has taken you almost thirty-five years to coax it towards a design you are almost happy with. Most days, nothing aches anymore. There is a dancer's strength in your legs (satisfying, although you still cannot dance). Your back finally has that little furrow down the spine, instead of a devilish bony ridge. (*Fuller*, your wife calls this, meaning bloodgutter, meaning the groove swaged into a dagger.) In recent years, you've taken to wearing bold, striking garments, no longer made anxious by the unsolicited admiration of strangers, of being pulled up in the street to receive praise. But how much of this is your wife's doing?

And how much, the idea that the (heavily abridged) rustlings of your unquiet mind might amount to a creditable profession?

You make people up, she'll reason. Why not do that more thoroughly? You know, flesh and blood. Cellular differentiation, she'll add, in attempt to suffuse these words with undeserved magic.

You have seen me with plants, you might argue. You have seen me with sourdough culture, and goldfish . . . (Here you might provide her with a litany of minor deaths, deficiencies of care. Up to and including the indoor pomegranate tree, which you forgot to take out of doors—for rain and for light—before taxiing to the airport, and whose expensive leafless corpse will be the first thing to greet you upon return: Welcome home.)

Somehow, these various failures, rather than exonerating you, only strengthen her resolve: parenthood will temper you. You will become the kind of person who habitually spritzes maidenhairs and sparrow orchids, monitoring direct lines of sun and ambient humidity.

I don't want to be quiet of mind, you'll say.

What the hell are you talking about? she'll say.

Fine, you'll tell her. But if we're using my body, we're using my eggs.

Well, that's just selfish.

It's economical. More ethical, really, if you consider medical resources—are you considering medical resources?

Then it wouldn't be ours; it would just be yours. Biologically.

Is this a legality thing? you'll ask. I'm not to be trusted? You have it, then.

But there is the real and legitimate concern of how many real-life people depend upon your wife being properly slept and reasonably nourished, capable of making clear and imperishable arguments, in order to ensure the equitable pursuit of their own lives, the lives of their preexisting, nonhypothetical children.

What you could say, the noncombustible truth, if you were brave enough to offer it: Lover, I am afraid.

What you say instead: I am not just going to incubate. Yes, you heard me. If you want to secure your bloodline so desperately . . .

The argument follows more or less the same trajectory each run-through, typically culminating in each of you affecting to want a child a little less than the other, a little less than whatever might demand sacrifice in your life, lives.

Fine, she said, this morning, in the room with no view of the lake. I've still got a few years to work it out.

Age. She has years left, you do not. What used to be called a trump card, and now must be called an ace.

In the meantime, it's not like you're using your body for anything remarkable.

The same attributes that made your wife a formidable fighter have made her a proficient lawyer. She is not a malicious person. There is no terrible force that charges through her veins, darkening her blood. Her blood simply quickens, at will, with acute direction and purpose. Her ferocity follows a higher fluency, is meticulously checked and metered.

When her nose was busted for the second time, busted legitimately, she hung up her gloves without resentment. Some score had been settled—it wasn't for others (for you) to understand. She was twenty-seven anyway. Time to lift her gaze beyond the ropes.

When you were twenty-seven, you spent most of your time appraising the lurid vinyl wallpaper of your sister's caravan in rural South Australia, listening to snakes nesting behind the flat tires while you waited for the benzodiazepine to kick in, because there is no version of your life (*better*, *best*, or otherwise) in which your own blood does not darken with a terrible force. That would be someone else's life altogether.

Your wife is built of sturdier stuff. Unperturbable. She could run on fumes for miles, days. Across the micro-universe of the diner table, she's finally holding your gaze. Enough of an olive branch. What is it that makes the eyes appear to gain or recover lucency? She would tell you it's a misperception, merely the ambient light.

She settles the bill, paying from the envelope of U.S. twenties her mother gave the two of you as an eloping gift—*Here's to shared debt!*

You leave, two hands for the coffee. All that is needed now is to put a little distance, a couple of hundred miles between yourselves and the room with no view of the lake, and the things that were said within it.

Otherwise, the river, the mist and geese traveling along it at varying elevations, varying speeds, southward. Otherwise, a townie child in a blue knit cap standing atop a Hollywood-red hydrant, demanding to be carried. Otherwise, the lozenge-colored leaves adorning the hire car. The vertiginous feeling of the cold snap in your lungs, of being out of season.

You set the coffee on the car roof and hold your hands up for the keys.

Your wife hesitates on the passenger side. But can't we wait? she asks. Walk around a bit, spend a little more of this sun? We won't beat the dark, anyway—it'll be dark by the time we get on the Taconic.

For now, at least, the sky is the same blue as the plastic stretched drum-tight over the boats in the yacht club lot, over names you try to guess, wandering quietly through their ranks—*Hortensia*, *Wilhelmina*, *Boondoggle*—voices low, as though these vessels might stir from their wintering and unwittingly crush you. *Loose lips list ships.* The yacht club road veers right where it meets the river, becomes gravel, becomes grassy ruts and NO TRESPASSING, water to one side, woods to the other, ramparted by raspberry canes and poison ivy receding from the cold. She goes ahead, holding most of the branches from whipping back into your face. She is dressed too lightly for this weather, but doesn't show it. Discomfort of any kind—fear, pain, guilt, embarrassment—is an animal she keeps separate from herself. Something she can leave outside and neglect to feed.

You watch her moving along the trail. Her rangy grace, a sighthound's lope. In your smaller moments, you are envious of her narrow shoulders, her boyish hips. With men, had you ever appreciated such things without envy? Hard to remember. With her it has been there from the first, though from the first she has forbidden such comparisons between yourselves. Seven years ago (whose party?) she was wearing a dress like slow liquid, a dark rippling fabric that feigned sliding off her at every slight turn. You complimented the dress by saying you could never get away with it. She laughed and said of course, of course you could.

You countered with all the reasons you could not—your proportions, your skin tone . . .

But your future wife cut you off, her face stony. No, she said. This is not what we do. This is not how we get close to each other, by making ourselves seem defective enough to safely befriend.

You'd thought a person would have to be drunk to be so

forthright. She was clear-eyed. You almost apologized, but stifled the urge.

Here, she offered, more gently. A few years ago I realized I'd stopped smiling in a way that hid my teeth. Now you go, your turn.

You told her that you had, at one point, truly hated your feet. What about them, exactly, you couldn't recall. Only that you'd taken considerable measures to keep them hidden. But somewhere along the way, you must've stopped thinking about them. Here they were now, exposed, in open-toe sling-backs. Apparently innocuous.

There, that's a start, she said, and sweetly bit your elbow. She had, you noticed with some annoyance, perfect teeth.

On the trail between woods and river you say little, and she less. But you pass through the same nets of oaky light, stumble over the same surfaced roots, muddy your city boots with the same forest-river mud. Something is lifting, being forgiven, by one or the both of you. Something is being resolved at a microbial level, being silently disassembled and carted away like a threatening foreign mass under an army of tiny diligent claws. It is enough, it is more than enough. You could go like this till dark and through it, wordlessly content. If it were warmer you might suggest a quick tumble in the poison ivy. But then the path opens into a clearing, littered with signs of use or misuse: half-buried plastic five-gallon, rusty propane tank, old ribbed-glass bottles, many beer and soda cans with ring-pulled mouths gaping in a style discontinued in the seventies or eighties. You kick through the strata of fallen leaves for any proof of the new millennium, of more recent visitors, but no.

Time slip, your wife says knowingly. The Catskills are full of them. I've read about it. Service stations that appear once and never again, where a tank of fuel costs six dollars and you can still buy RC Cola and Kamel Reds.

It won't show up on film, then? you ask, reaching for your phone.

In pixels, you mean? You can try, but I bet your Instagram crashes.

It's then that you notice the woman, standing on a narrow flank of pebbled beach, looking out across the river. Her lichen-colored parka is modern enough, Dry-Tek or somesuch. She does nothing to acknowledge she's heard you. How has she not heard you?

She has come here to howl, to howl unhindered; you know this before she opens her lungs and begins to do so. The sound agonied, agonizing. And though you cannot know the root of the anguish, it is familiar to you. From the town, through the trees, the sound of bells. She has timed her bawling to the church bells, meaning, perhaps, that she has done this before, done this often. For how long has she done this—months? Years? Her hood is up, but she cannot be much older than your wife, than yourself. She has smooth, slender hands that are taut now, fingers splayed as though they too are emitting sound, or light. Terrible force.

Shouldn't we see if—

But your wife touches her fingers to your wrist. She has a certain grace with grief, the grief of others. You have seen this, received it. She presses her palm flat between your shoulder blades and you turn together, away, back the way you came, towards the bells, walking abreast when the trail allows.

Dusk seeps from the ground up, obliterating the woods. A desperate, newly hollowed feeling, a draining away. In a neighboring life, you're the woman in the lichen-colored coat, howling towards god-knows-what across the water, elegant hands rigid with pain.

Hey, you plead silently. Look at me.

Your wife turns, as if you've spoken. The last of the light. This morning, in the first of it: her crooked nose, her troubled brow, the glint of her still perfect teeth between her ragged lips. Here we are, you'd thought then, a fact at once miraculous and not, a deer appearing in a frozen salvage yard at midnight, tiptoeing between the moonlit wrecks.

And now, in this riverside town at the edge of the road map, watching your wife pull her coat to her chin in the passenger seat, you're thinking it again: Here we are. An astonishment common to any love. Your blood quiet. A day in which you made the best of what little light there was, the first and last of it on your love's face.

With eyes still closed she says, You're watching me, aren't you? I can tell. Stop watching me.

You want me to stop watching you?

No.

Okay.

As you flick the headlights up, the question arrives from somewhere outside your own questioning, more scent or frequency than language: *When was the last time you wished for different?* And the answer will be a very long way from reach.

Sinkers

At thirty-three he goes back to the town his mother was raised in. She'd taken him there as a child every summer, for her own birthday, and they'd rowed out in a hired tinny to eat a picnic above the place she believed her house must have been. Must still be. The doorstep, at least, which had been made of concrete, and maybe the skeleton of the house itself, many years drowned, its brick chimney home to nests of eels and whorls of trout.

I was born down there, she'd tell him, again and again between mouthfuls of egg sandwich and swigs of portello. And when I was fourteen the Hydroelectric came, so we all had to leave.

He'd looked out over the side of the little boat, into the green depths, and imagined his mother being hauled up out of them. Reeled like a fish to the surface, into the dry boring world, gleaming and furious and fighting the air. He imagined his father was down there too, though likely the man had never seen the town, or even the lake that had swallowed it. Still, he was somehow there, doing father things—tending to lake weeds instead of lawn, shaving his jaw, leaning over the underwater sink to stare at his reflection in the underwater mirror, his features made bleary by the gray-green murk of the government-ordained lake. Cristian had never known his father's face. Not even the picture of it. His mother had never tried to chase this stranger down, knew he wouldn't have stayed in any case. It didn't matter, she said. She had everything she needed.

Does he even know about me?

Cricket, how could he?

There was no truth she meant to protect him from.

Look, kiddo, other people are going to lie to you. And some are going to do it out of what they think is kindness. Not me, though, I'm never going to. You might as well get used to it.

At the boat hire, Cristian buys three hours from the man who has run the shed for the past two decades, and likely before. Cristian recalls seeing him there, all through the nineties—hair a little less wild then, a little less white—bringing the boats in or directing them out, otherwise leaning in the shaded doorway of the hire shed, perpetually in the act of rolling a cigarette he never seemed to get around to smoking. He's doing so now, licking the gummed edge and letting it hang on his lip, unlit, a thin cocoon dangling from a ledge. He lumbers bearlike across the dock, looks down at Cristian's suede oxfords, up at his stiff-collared shirt—Just get outter church?—and leads him to a silver tinny, unhitching it with an *in-ya-get*.

Cristian knows he's thinking *tourist*, with that curdled feeling of contempt and relief. It's mostly tourists who hire, tourists who bring in money. On the jetty two children squat to stare into the buckets of live bait while their father threads their hand reels, socking hooks with wormflesh as he explains about the bells. It's a story Cristian has overheard many times before; that if you stick your head under at just the right hour, you'll hear the old church bells ringing.

His mother had had no patience for that sort of thing.

They don't know what the hell they're talking about. The church was shifted out along with everything else. Stick your head under the water, she used to say, and all you're going to hear is your ears getting wet.

She'd told him other stories, better stories. What she called the *true* Provost stories. Of how the new town appeared to remember the old, and over the years had inched down the mountainside, trying to sneak back to it. Of weekends spent watching boys free-dive the drowned town, rowing out with rocks they'd use as sinkers, tipping over the sides with them hugged tight to their chests so they'd reach the bottom fast and easy, wouldn't waste any time or breath getting down there.

It gave them longer to look around, she said.

Look around for what?

Oh, they just wanted to see for themselves. They wanted to get deep enough to look in the windows of the houses that got left behind. Like there were people still down there living watery ghost lives or something. Sitting down to breakfast at the table like normal, but when you pour out the cereal it just goes everywhere like fish food. That's what they wanted to see, things like that.

Cristian unlaces his shoes and peels his damp socks from his feet, his shins white from the Sydney winter, from too many months lived under office fluorescents. He has brought no food, no water, just the old biscuit tin and its sifting contents. He stows it on one of the slat seats, rosellas and gum blossoms encircling the rim. Glinting. A bright day for August. Still the dark will come early, sun already stippled through gum branches. He pushes off from the jetty with outstretched arms, oars slipping in the locks.

The boatman peering from his shade, shaking his head and muttering something under his breath—*paper pusher* or *yuppie poofter*—though without much in the way of vitriol. Finally, turning away.

No wind in the valley, the lake doubling everything faithfully. Bathysphere. Ghost gums twinned from their roots, branching towards alternate skies. Nothing to trouble that second world but the wakes of a few wading birds, and that of himself, dipping the oar blades towards their reflections without much rhythm or effect. He is no good with the oars. No good with his arms. The children's voices are still clear and his palms already hot.

His mother. Out there on the water she'd looked glamorous. Even rowing, her forehead creased with the effort of sawing the oars back and forth, and the humidity pressing her fine hair flat. Her dress would be tucked up to keep from the slimy water sloshing in the bottom of the boat. The end of the eighties, the beginning of the nineties—somehow she'd escaped that era's synthetic epidemic, dressing always in linen, pale silk, soft things that would crease and show stains if you were that kind of person. She was not.

Crimplene's just another word for lazy, she said, as if he had any idea what crimplene was.

Sometimes she'd rowed them out over the house where a man had maybe killed his wife and child, or maybe not. It had been a talky sort of town, she said, and that talk just seemed to increase with the altitude after the relocation. The town had been flooded the year after the girl and her mother were found dead in their kitchen. No one ever said how. Too awful, was the only answer that parents would give. Too awful to talk about, perhaps because they did not really know, and the rumors were outrageous and conflicting. Something about poison, but whose fault, and maybe an accident after all?

Most people's houses were trucked out of the valley, up the side of the mountain. But that house was either too rickety or too sad, and it stayed where it was. The roof tiles were salvaged but the rest was left to the flood. Cristian's mother's house got left behind as well, feasted on by white ants to which Cristian's grandfather had been happy enough to surrender a three-year battle, knowing the termites' mingy victory would be short-lived.

It was the other house, the roofless, too-awful-to-talk-about house that the boys were diving down to. Hugging stones to their chests all those years ago. Sometimes they'd surface with things held between their teeth or tucked into the pockets and belt loops of their cut-down denims. Things they called *evidence*: rusted cutlery, a brown glass bottle, medicinal or sinister. Someone said that if you pulled up the waterlogged floorboards you'd find—what? *Proof.* Of what? *You know. How he. You know.* And when they couldn't bring back proof they'd surface with stories. *Something down there. Something grabbed me. Swam past two shadows in the doorway. Swear it, then. I swear.*

She'd known the daughter, of course. Emily. Hair short and soft and black as cat's fur. And her teeth when she laughed were like a cat's, small and sharp. The two had clattered over the town's corrugated dirt streets on boys' bicycles. Tearing pages out of Great-grandmother's leather-bound King James and daring each other to eat them.

And the doors shall be shut in the streets, when the sound of the grinding is low, and he shall rise up at the sound of the bird . . .

Was that it? His mother had shivered, out there above the town. Em said Ecclesiastes tasted best.

He has come with no water, no food. An ache in his fillings for the store-bought cake his mother took out to the lake each year; fake cream, icing shiny and hard like a beetle's back. Nothing close to what she could have made herself, but she thought it bad luck for a person to bake their own birthday cake, and his efforts would have been a clotted mess. They would take their sandwich crusts and empty drink bottles home with them, but they'd crumble up some of the cake and scatter it over the side like rice at a wedding. Watch the white sugary sponge dissolve into the lake water, splashing away any fish or ducks who tried to paddle in and eat it.

Not for you. Not for you.

This is what he remembers, looking towards the smooth trunks of ghost gums at the lake's edge, hoping for something familiar, something that might act as a point of reference. There is no such thing. Even the boat shed is gone from sight, and there is nothing to indicate whether or not this is the right place. The lake tells him little, dumbly reflecting back the deepening sky. Cristian takes the lid from the biscuit tin, sees the powder and bone gravel, and cannot do it. He gives himself a minute to recover his nerve, thinks he could maybe drop the entire tin over the side. But this is worse somehow—he can't explain it, even to himself—like burying someone alive.

Cricket, can you just do as you're asked?

But alone on the lake he feels helpless. Stranded. He opens and closes the tin, unable to look at its contents. He opens and closes his fists. From a great distance he watches his trembling, overscrubbed hands fumble the lid off the tin. Okay, he says to the hands. Okay. But they scramble to close it up again.

Her body was tiny when she finally slipped out of it. When he'd gone to collect the ashes, he had thought there must have been a mistake, because what they gave him couldn't have filled a coffee jar. But she'd always been a little thing; where was there room for a tumor? No one knew how her body had hidden it, a growth the size of a clementine. Kept it secret until it was too late.

Why do they always measure cancer by fruit, she'd wanted to know. Why always citrus?

Well. Orange you glad it wasn't a grapefruit?

It had exhausted him to even think it, let alone say it aloud, but there was the sound of her laugh, her real laugh with the huskiness it had acquired since she'd started therapy. They were in her backyard that afternoon, under the loquat tree, the fallen fruit soft and rotting under their shoes. The air was boozy with ferment, and the effects of the chemo weren't yet too visible. She sat in a dining chair, a blue towel draped around her shoulders. It might have been a moment in which to pretend things were otherwise. But she'd seen the other patients around the ward, their hair falling out in great drifts, and decided that wasn't for her.

You'll do it? she'd asked. I'm tired of all these strangers touching me. I just don't have the patience for it anymore. I've never really had the patience for anyone else, but now I'm excused from pretending.

She had held her hand out for the clippers and adjusted the setting, then handed them back to him. Just give me a number three. It's all going to go anyway.

He'd started underneath, at her nape, so if she changed her mind they could rescue it to something less drastic. But she stared straight ahead as the shoulder-length tresses of copper blond fell into the grass around their feet. He was thinking that he should save some, remembering the envelopes of baby curls she'd kept, the date and his age in months noted in blue biro. But that kind of keepsaking didn't belong to the deep end of life. It would look morbid. Unhopeful. He left the hair where it fell, two inches of pale gray already showing at the roots. Two inches, what did that amount to in weeks? Five or six? That was how long ago she'd given up on hair dye. She put her hand up to check his progress, brushing fingertips over the soft stubble.

Isn't it funny, she said. It's what I used to give you.

He had turned off the clippers, leaving her with a fine, fox-silver fuzz that rubbed away over the following weeks, until she was a vulnerable, newborn-looking creature, but with sharpened, haunted features. She lived long enough to see it grow back, a darker gray, in tight, dense curls. Then something had gotten into her chest, fluid on the lungs, and she didn't have the strength left to fight it off.

He's late bringing the boat back, the unemptied biscuit tin balanced on his knees. As he rows into shore he can see the blue doors of the boat shed have been pulled closed, the buckets of live bait gone from the jetty. He docks and bangs a few times, openhanded, on the side of the shed. Inside there is radio noise, talk at commentary speed, but he can't make out the sport. Something from the daylit side of the globe.

Then the sound of a bolt sliding, and the boatman opens the door, chest hair sprouting from the low neck of his navy singlet.

I'm sorry, Cristian says. Late.

I see that. He looks Cristian up and down, for the second time that day, his eyes coming to rest on the biscuit tin tucked under Cristian's arm. Hopeful, maybe, for the offer of a Monte Carlo.

Cristian starts to explain but the man just nods like he's seen it all before. Putting it all together—the good shoes, the absence of fishing gear—placing him. The younger man feels more grateful than he'd care to admit, being placed.

How'd you go, then, get everyone home?

Cristian shakes his head. I owe you extra, he offers. I was out there another hour, at least.

Nah you don't. Not for you and she. You come in here for a tic.

He leads Cristian into the boat shed, under low-hanging bulbs in safety cages and past the rows of upturned boats in hibernation, awaiting trout season.

The man doesn't give his name and Cristian doesn't ask it, but he accepts a sweating can of beer and lowers himself into a folding chair. The surrounding walls are lined with shelves, and these are buckling with their load of old manuals and fishing guides, pages crenulated and thickening in the damp, and with rusty souvenirs dredged up from the old town.

Some years earlier a drought sucked half the lake away, and the town rose right up out of the mud like a sludgy, shipwormed beast. Former residents returned to tread gingerly across the lakebed, old shoes breaking through the thin, brittle layer baked over the softer, rich mud. From this they unearthed the detritus of their own histories. Things not worth the taking three decades earlier had appreciated down there in the silt, and people fished out bicycle parts, letter boxes, typewriter keys, the iron frame of an upright piano. Then the rains came back and the town was swallowed again.

Here are the photographs and newspaper clippings, tacked along the boat shed wall, mildew blooming under the glass frames. The height of the drought, the townspeople picking over the lakebed like prospectors.

His mother is there amongst them. Like all the rest she'd put on old shoes and walked right out over the cracked mud, across the not-lake. Right up to the empty windows of that too-awful house to see if the table was still set. All she saw, she said, was a roomful of rocks.

Come on, then, the boatman says—Are we going? Are we all set?—and Cristian hauls himself up from the chair to follow. Outside the air is cool and heavy, the viscosity of water, and it can no longer be said where the lake and the night divide, moon slapping boat flank as if to say *Go on go on go on*. Here is a charge now, a change in the air. A resonance. Whatever comes after a bell has rung out and the sound has drifted away.

Post-Structuralism for Beginners

It's not something they always do, not as if they can't get anywhere without watching it. Months might pass without any mention of the tape. But then it will appear again. Like the weights set or the pantry moths, it's seasonal. The pattern and duration of these seasons typically determined by Aland, with the latest being particularly lengthy. The Seven-Month Winter of the Tape. He hauled the VCR out of the cupboard while the boys were away over Easter, and it still hasn't gone back. School camps, football camps, sleepovers, grandparent visits—whenever Josh and Avery are out of the house overnight, Johanna can sense the tape lying in wait. Just the sight of the boys' overnight kit waiting in the hallway conjures a strange cocktail of dread and sexual guilt.

Across the hall, she can hear Aland dragging furniture around in the bedroom, setting up. *Deck chairs on the* Titanic, she thinks, bracing herself for the timid knock against her study door. There.

When she goes in, he's already sitting at the end of the bed, shuffling off his jeans. Two glasses of scotch wait dumbly on the bedside tables. She drops down next to her husband, unbuttoning her shirt as the VCR swallows the tape. There is the machine shudder, the awful grinding noise, and there *she* is. Ta-da. Cheekbones like a straight-edge razor and a degree in cultural studies that will not arm her for the world in the way she hopes it might.

On tape, she is twenty-three and he is just about to turn twenty-six. She has shocking tan lines from a week on Great Keppel Island, the outline of her bikini bottoms stark and sharp as if marked out by painters' tape. He has them too, encircling his thighs and hips, but they don't look as ridiculous against his darker skin, and in any case she has the lion's share of screen time. Alone at first, bending over that ostentatious desk he used to work from. Then he's there, or at least his hands are, spreading her legs wider for the camera, toying with the zoom. All of this happens silently. The camera was new then, a wedding gift sent from his uncle in Soweto. Aland couldn't get the sound to work, and she can't remember what they might have said to each other in those first few years. Sometimes she imagines her own soundtrack:

How's that? You like that?

Yes.

Yes?

Yes.

She is really much better at smuggling post-structuralism into real estate listings.

Johanna wonders if she should feel flattered, relieved. There is something almost faithful about it, the way he returns to this snowy anachronism when the internet is a glut of high-definition eighteen-year-olds with vaginas like baci di dama, rose macarons.

The original Beta cassette had been labeled "Home Maintenance Tips," to preemptively bore potential browsers, but also as a nod to the use of electrical tape. God alone knows where that copy is now. The VHS recording is labeled "Post-Structuralism for Beginners," in the hope that if their sons ever find its hiding place (camouflaged with some old textbooks in a box at the top of the wardrobe) while in search of Christmas presents or cigarettes, they won't be remotely tempted to watch. Would they even recognize these mute amateurs as their mother and father? They would, yes. Behind the unsettling boxcar mustache, beneath the boho-rococo hair and makeup, she and Aland are clearly, indefensibly themselves.

Despite the care at concealment, she knows the boys will

likely find and watch the tape anyway, just as she had found and watched her own parents' pornography. This was the natural order of things. Although the videos Johanna and her sister discovered had mercifully featured actors, who were beautiful and experienced and, more important, were not their parents. That was in the eighties, before hate-sex was invented, when porn stars still had pubic hair and even double penetration appeared affectionate.

She worries for her boys, growing up with the internet, the unreasonable promises it makes. The axing of plot lines, however—the disappearance of cruise ships and card games and pool cleaners—she envies them that much.

Aland finishes before the tape does, and they lie there together, Johanna tracing pragmatic circles to bring herself unceremoniously across the line while the last several minutes of footage grind along. The racier parts have been rewound so many times that her orgasm happens in a soundless blizzard.

We should really get this digitized, Aland says. Before it gets any worse.

Sure. We'll just drop it off at the lab where Michelle's son works.

Hah, he says. The sound of a laugh but it isn't, really. Over the past few years it's as if he's been slowly smuggling himself into his work, away from her. The harder she looks at him, the less she recognizes. She imagines him leaving the house each morning with pieces of himself hidden in his shoes, his coat lining, folded up small between the pages of his lecture notes and macroeconomics textbooks. Quietly liberating his humor, his intuition, his capacity for real discussion. She wonders where he's hoarding it all. At faculty functions she's watched the undergraduates, sooty eyes and lamé tights, turning their delicate wrists towards her husband. When had macroeconomics students become so desirable, so *female*? She listens to them soft-soaping Aland with questions about Bitcoin mining and the cost of Peugeots in Cuba, trying to detect whether there's some kind of cute sexual undercurrent.

She'd been around that age, an undergraduate when they met. But politically oblivious, dumb as carpet. Someone else—some marketing reptile—was trying to get her hammered on Compound Fractures at the Union. But it was Aland she stalked around the bar, backed by the volatile concoction of brandy and champagne, an idiot for his accent. *Effrica? Come on, tell me something else about Effrica*, till he banged down his pint and said he'd had quite enough of that. She could either kiss him or kiss off.

What's your name then? Johanna? Hah. The town where I was born . . .

Who remembers what else was said, and it's likely better not—what did she even know about South Africa, at that age, save Fraser handing Mandela a Bradman-signed cricket bat? And a boy at high school who'd informed her that, Back There, if someone hurts an animal or a woman, they place a tire around his neck. *And then they burn the tire.*

She hadn't even known enough to ask who "they" were.

Aland had been, all considered, very patient with her.

Just lucky you're beautiful, he'd say, when she'd said or done something dim. Though not in recent memory. And she had never looked like these girls, like his students.

Johanna rolls off the bed, trapping the thought like a spider under an upturned glass. Leaving it there to deal with later, when she's built up enough nerve to either stomp on the thing or release it, depending on how dangerous she decides it might be.

Aland has fallen asleep, or fallen silent, as he so often does after sex, a forearm blocking his eyes from light.

She steals the top sheet away and wraps it around herself, and goes back to her study to read over a draft for a listing:

If we tear down a haunted building, are its ghosts dispatched with it? And if so, at what point during renovations might we encounter the divergence of the two, of these concrete and spectral histories? This former deviation heterotopia exemplifies an harmonious conversion from the institutional to the domestic; a wholly inhabitable space which remains architecturally sympathetic to the original structure and its prominence in Australian cultural mythology.

It had been suggested Johanna "play down the whole former-prison thing," and she'd obliged, despite realizing years ago that the sub-editors at *The Leader* never actually read her real estate features. That probably no one read her real estate features; they just scanned the number of bedrooms and bathrooms and otherwise referred to the photographs, if not the internet. This had become apparent while she was carrying

Josh—a troublingly synesthetic pregnancy, the likely spark for a tangential article about the taste and mouthfeel of Usonian architecture: *a slightly scorched, malty characteristic with lingering notes of tobacco and undertones of nutmeg and poached pome fruit*. It ran, and the house sold at 200K above estimate, which may have had something or nothing at all to do with Johanna's culinary digression. The listings have become her own feeble joke with herself, a way of keeping her hand in. As long as she sticks to word count and conjures a woeful pun in reference to the street name, she has free artistic license to poach liberally from De Certeau and Foucault, to weave in knowledge she no longer has any practical use for. (Secretly, she hopes that somewhere out there, in a cultural backwater not so very far away, some retired semiotics professor is at least getting a kick out of them.)

Johanna saves the article as *Your Big Break?* and shuts her laptop.

Then she opens it again. What does she even mean by *wholly inhabitable*?

In the morning she wakes cotton-mouthed, wet light sluicing through the blinds. Aland hours gone. Down the length of her body, past the rumpled lenticular of the bed linen, there's the blank gray face of the television, VCR beneath it, tape poking out like a tongue.

Does she hate the tape? She hates the tape. She sometimes fantasizes about the tape's destruction, at her own hands or at the hands of fate. Watching it seems a grim suburban cousin to the ouroboric punishments dealt out in Greek mythologies. There are accidents she might orchestrate, catastrophes that could conceivably befall the tape. It could simply go missing; Aland might presume it was the boys and be too embarrassed to ask them. The content could be buried irretrievably beneath layers of Winter Olympic curling highlights and sub-Saharan carnivore documentaries. Or she could just forget the subterfuge and gut the thing, crack it open and unravel its innards. Wind the slick black ribbons around the bedposts and wait for him to say something. She has even considered a new tape, them as they are now, but is haunted off such a plaintive attempt at lust revival by a scene in a novel read two decades ago—Edith(?) covered top to toe in red greasepaint, lying naked on the lounge room floor and imploring the protagonist: *Let's pretend we're other people.* It does not go very well, or sexily. After being rebuffed, Edith(?) curls up in the bottom of an elevator shaft and is crushed to death.

Johanna shuts the blinds and feeds the tape to the VCR. More and more, she finds she is not looking at the parts she's supposed to be looking at. Instead she is searching the minutiae of the room—the grain of the desk and the pattern in the wallpaper, the smudges around the light switch—for clues as to what the rest of their life looks like. Their younger life. There is the door, but she can't recall much about the hallway beyond it. Was this the house with the outdoor laundry, the blighted lemon tree? The eccentric landlord who would turn up unannounced in the backyard with a bucket and a lemon-reaching device he'd fashioned himself from a broomstick and an empty Coke can? Yes. And a kitchen that smelled of overripe oranges, for no reason they could ever determine. Unable to find the hogo's source, there was nothing to do but keep a steady supply of oranges to account for it. Piling them into a clay bowl in the middle of the table and leaving them to soften and sprout fuzz. Aland weeded out the more deflated of them with good-humored disgust: There are times I've mistaken you for a rational woman.

She rewinds the tape and watches again, nearly the whole way through, trying to see beyond what the camera has recorded, what is imprinted there in the layers of emulsion. But even the things that have been captured in-frame are unreliable. Her body is not that body. The house has probably been torn down. On tape, Aland still has the tiny asterisk of a scar on his cheek, from a cop's signet ring. But the scar has long since faded, absorbed by the body. Even the camera is gone now, stolen during a road trip, and the film is deteriorating with each view. *Remanence decay—a process in which the magnetic particles gradually lose their charge, resulting in colors shifting towards weaker hues.* (Comes the absurd thought: Are we doing this to ourselves?)

Through the decaying film she glimpses a sliver of the decaying garden; decaying even at the time of filming. Benign neglect. It has been one of Aland's few stipulations: there must always be a backyard. No matter how small or shabby or overgrown; no matter how seldom he'll go out into it to get his hands dirty or fail at vegetables. Corollary of his childhood. *The Great Indoors*—his mother's term for the period of years (six? seven?) she'd had to keep Aland inside, hidden from authorities and conservative snoops, his very existence a violation of South Africa's Immorality Amendment Act. As it was, she'd been spat on more than once, assaulted in the street by women and men both. She now enjoyed scandalizing docile Australians with stories of routine panty raids on those suspected of interracial love, police storming the house and shaking out the bedsheets. Tipping out the wash-basket to scrutinize underwear for signs of unlawful union.

People told me I should abort, Aland's mother had told Johanna. And when I refused they said I should lie, cry rape. Poor little white Norna! But that would've hardly helped anyone's cause, neither in the short nor long term. We figured better to lie low for a while. You could feel the wind turning, by then. Or we had to believe we did.

Like one long rainy day, those years, Norna and her sister trying to make a game of it, inventing distractions that didn't bore the three of them senseless—*Do you remember Magic Linen Press? Breakfast circus?*—while friends were arrested for civil disobedience, high treason, disappeared into exile or simply disappeared. Aland had been allowed into the garden only, when deemed safe. A grassy cubby amidst watchful strelitzia at the end of the yard represented the outer limits of his child-world.

When recalling his childhood for their sons, Aland cloaked it in a near magical allure, as though his cloistered upbringing was a nefarious enchantment, the consequence of some foul sorcery. The more complex version, he insisted, could wait.

Something crashes outside, in the garden. In the off-screen, present-day, presently decaying garden. Johanna pauses the tape, and listens.

. . . *the smallest parcel of the world and then it is the totality of the world* . . . Foucault, trailing her out through the back door, like a sat-nav she can't turn off.

There is a shudder in the Photinia hedge, where it separates their block from the back neighbors, and Johanna crosses the lawn to meet it. She trails her hand along the hedge, the young red leaves sun-warmed and tender, slightly clammy under her palm, like the hide of a living animal. She parts the leaves and peers through the cool shadowy network of branches.

A man in gardener's greens, his old face shaded by a slouch hat, hacking at the branches on the other side with diligent whacks of a machete, his own hands gnarled as tree matter.

This is how Aland's father would sometimes visit him. Appearing in broad daylight, in the dusty blue cottons of a groundsman, during the Great Indoors. (Although Norna maintains that this is simply not possible: she was watching the whole time. She did recall a phase, however, when he thought all black men were Sifiso.)

But Aland described the meetings in such vivid and consistent detail—the deep burnished *hurng hurgh hurgh* of his father's laugh, his genius for bird and animal mimicry, the tiny stick-and-poke tattoo of a date (Aland's birthday?) on the inside of his right wrist—that Johanna was compelled to believe him. Sometimes even Norna looked swayed.

It wasn't your birthday, that tattoo, she once interrupted

cagily. It was the first day of the Soweto uprising. You must've heard Aunt Flossie and me talking about it.

This is the reason, Johanna suspects, for there always being a backyard: so that Aland's father, apparition or no, might have favorable conditions in which to reappear.

And now here he is, after all, come to wreak havoc on the Photinia.

Excuse me? she asks through the hedge.

The man pauses work to raise his head, face appearing under the brim of his slouch hat. Not him. Of course, not him. Barely older than Johanna, and white—if a very weathered white, the hands extending from his shirt cuffs worked even darker, older.

Hello—yeah?

Why are you whacking up our Photinia?

That how you say it? Owners are selling. Reckon a fence will market better than a hedge, I s'pose. People are very fond of their fences.

But it's on our side too. Or half of it is. It's a common hedge.

Same owners, but. Whole-hedge prerogative.

Oh. Johanna hadn't known this. In fact, she's never met the owners, only the estate agent, or a rolling cast of them, snipping through the house for half-yearly inspections.

Could you not just . . . trim it back on that side and put the fence in front of it?

It'd only grow back and wreck the fence. The roots, you see . . .

I see.

Sorry, love. You still got some running up the sides there.

Not his fault, Johanna thinks, stalking back to the house. Not his fault, not his fault. She scrapes a white plastic chair onto the paving stones and watches a shaggy window appear in the hedge. The window becomes a doorway, the gardener steps into it, notices Johanna sitting there, gives a self-conscious little bow, rolls up his sleeves, and gets back to it.

Johanna, not wanting to unsettle him with her attention, goes inside for a book and a mug of tea, returns to the chair, affects to be taking the afternoon sun, which has grown toothy, vengeful in the wake of the morning's storm, searing the wet off the grass in green bright steam.

She watches the gardener from the periphery of an Icelandic thriller. Over the course of the afternoon the hedge becomes less a solid wall than a recalcitrant old stage curtain being roughly thrust aside.

At one point she calls out to offer a cold drink, but he raises a thermos as if in toast. She raises her peppermint tea in reply. The crinkling around his eyes, the work-roughened hands, the fur on his arms. His chest and belly, she imagines, similarly furred—not a thing she's ever thought of as being *her* thing, but perhaps she could. Very D. H. Lawrence. But after the apparition of Aland's father it would feel warped, unseemly. Freud would say . . .

Well, fuck Freud to Whitsunday.

The rain returns. The gardener throws a look at the sky, expression hidden by hat brim, then returns to clawing up the Photinia's root system.

Johanna, subterfuge lost, leaves the book on the arm of the chair and goes inside. Two texts on her phone from Aland, in reverse order:

I'll take that as a No then.

And the first, an hour earlier, letting her know that he and the boys were having dinner with his mother. *Want to join?*

Sorry, she texts back. *Headache*. She's considered leaving Aland only once before, children not yet pictured. Storming out of an argument and driving as far as Mount Baw Baw. Arriving in the St. Gwinear car park after sunset and sleeping all night in the driver's seat with her coat pulled up to her chin. It might have happened last century, it feels that long ago. In the morning, there it all was: mountains stereoscopic against Polaroid sky, extravagances people traveled great distances to be humbled by. But the ski season hadn't started yet and she was alone there. She'd rummaged through the glove compartment and discovered a chocolate bar and half a pack of Extra Milds that her friend Silv had stashed and forgotten about. Johanna had leaned against the car's flank, alternating mouthfuls of smoke and chocolate as she watched the mist lift. God, it was beautiful. Your whole life could be like this. Arriving always in darkness and waking to something extraordinary. You wouldn't even have to be rich. But she knew it couldn't be. She warmed the car and pointed it back towards Melbourne. All the lives she wasn't living lined up uselessly: tacky snow globes from places she had never been, places where it doesn't even snow.

In their bedroom the tape has started playing again, to nobody. How is this possible? Power surge, some other glitch, divine meddling. Johanna doesn't know. Unnerving, though. Again, the soundless scream, the confectioner's red-and-pink and of her mouth and sex. She wrenches the tape out of the VCR, hoping the ribbon might catch and unravel, absolving her, but of course it doesn't.

One more hour until Aland brings the boys back from his mother's. One more hour until they bound into the house, crashing from great sugary heights. Delivering covert kicks to each other's shins and staging vengeful stuffed-animal executions in protest of the sudden dearth of chocolate biscuits and unlimited television.

Johanna takes a marker from a kitchen drawer. She relabels the tape "Anatomy of Lesser-Known Knowns," then relabels it "Blank" and returns it to the company of dead French theorists.

Through the sliding doors she sees the hedge is no longer. In its place, a muddy trench, the remnants of Photinia swept into a tall brush pile halfway up the neighboring yard.

The gardener is kneeling on the grass, wiping his tools clean with a rag, packing them away. No suggestion of a fence, not an upright post in sight.

What about privacy? Johanna asks. Standing over him, furious now.

He looks up at her, from under his sodden hat. Long scratches raking his forearms, where the hedge had fought him back.

I've got a family to get home to, he says. You know, a life?

Of course, she says, eyes seeking the bottom of the trench.

I'll be back with the fence things tomorrow, he says. But you don't need to worry—there's no one living there now. It's all just set up for the auction.

She's still holding the VHS tape.

Haven't seen one of those for a while, he says, with a chuck of his chin.

Old art project, she says. Very pretentious.

Beauty over bread, hey? Still, nice if you can have both.

Yes, she says, warily, unsure if he's implying that she does have both.

Well, tomorrow. He nods. He gathers his things and strides up the lawn, a darkening green wave upon which the house floats, lit up like an ocean liner, the windows blazing.

She never paid much attention to this house while the Photinia was up, had little curiosity about the people who last lived there: childless, dogless, not inclined to parties. Though they sometimes ate their meals al fresco and listened to what sounded like Brubeck.

Eventide. Gloaming. Lustrous, lost words. Johanna strides towards the blazing windows, the house all the more adrift, and the wet of the grass soaking her cotton shoes. She leaves them neatly by the back door. Unlocked, unalarmed, nothing to keep her from the smooth cool of the slate floor underfoot, the museum echo of copious space. A house that is made to be moved through, calling her upstairs like a sleepy lover, but she doesn't. Bowl of hollow glass fruit on the table, the kitchen cupboards empty, the refrigerator lighting up on nothing, save somebody's half-finished bottle of coconut water. Johanna sets the VHS tape down on the black granite bench-top, turning the dimmer switch down to dark. She looks back across the churned strip of earth, to the meek light of her own home. The sliding door is still partly open. An echo of being six or seven, writing a goodbye note to her parents—*becos you dont care about me anymor*—packing a small bag for credibility's sake then hiding under the bed in the spare room, where she could monitor her mother and father's rising panic. How loudly her own heart pounded, pressed against the carpet.

They arrive home in heavy silver deluge. From the dark ship of the neighboring house, Johanna watches this diorama of her family, sons fighting their way out of raincoats and calling for her, room after room lighting up.

Only a frail guilt. Blown glass.

The back porch light comes on, in the house down the hill. Aland picks up the rain-soaked novel she'd been not-reading. Looking up he must notice the hedge, or the lack of it. His face is tilted towards the house, though it's obvious he can't see her, couldn't possibly see her, there in the dark.

She watches his mouth open silently around her name.

Chavez

For two weeks I have Maria's dog. For two weeks he wakes me by putting his large head on the bed and making his little howl-yawn to say he wants something—out, food, ear scratch—while Maria is down to the south fighting her mythological husband over their mythological children. No, this is not so fair of me, to say *mythological*. The children, I know, are not mythological. I have seen their photographs, tacked to the walls of Maria's studio apartment (colored lights to make it cheerful, paper chrysanthemums, unframed Kahlo prints, *bien sûr*). I went up there just one time, for one coffee, but I remember the photographs: the boy, the girl, both having glossy dark hair cut straight across their eyebrows. Their heights marked on the kitchen doorway, even though they have never stood there, I know, have never even placed their small feet into this city, or possibly this country.

And I have heard, many times, Maria's side of one same sad conversation—*Mi querido, why are you doing this? Don't do this to me*—which she has on the fire escape above mine. Again and again, *Por que? Por que?* and I watch her cigarette ash falling.

But of her family, only Chavez is real to me.

Maria adopted him when she first arrived here, and he was very small. He was snuffling outside a bakery like a bad cartoon of a lost dog, and she brought him home for company and also protection. Of course she was thinking forward, because at that size he could not have protected so much as a brioche. She named him Chavez, after this hero of the workers, but it is not a suitable name for him, I do not think. The human Chavez, as I recall, was quite wiry. Possibly from all the marching, and from being vegetarian. The canine Chavez seems made up of many pieces of different dogs, but the biggest piece is most certainly wolf, or something wolflike enough that he does not know how to bark; he can only howl and croon.

Maria had brought him to my door with her hand around his fraying collar, and they stood grinning together in the dim hallway. The same-shaped grin, it seemed to me, but with different things going on behind it. Maria: grateful, apologetic. Chavez: who knows? Still grinning, the two trotted into my kitchen, Maria in her too-high heels, her mongrel wolf-dog with his too-long toenails. Maria said to Chavez, *Escóndete!* and he looked around a moment before curling himself up beneath the table like a big polar doughnut, out of the way.

It is his best trick. She laughed. He understands he is *contrabando* in this lousy building.

Into my hand Maria pressed two folded bills to buy his food, and a key stamped DO NOT DUPLICATE, to access the apartment upstairs for toys and extra treats. Also the key for her mailbox.

So you are able to collect my speeding tickets, she said, though in truth she owns no car.

You are very good to do this, Séverine. Saturday twenty-fifth, I will be coming back. Then crouching down, a kiss for one of the dog's ears, she says she must catch her bus.

Then it is only myself and Chavez.

Until this time, I have only ever kept cats. I left the last one, Debbie Harry, for my sister-in-law Lotti to care for. I feel strangely embarrassed about this lack of dog knowledge.

Well, I say to Chavez, trying to sound casual. From under the table he looks at me (of course; who else would I be talking to?). What do you want? I ask.

Ouut, he says, in that yawn-howl. And in this moment I know that I have either been very smart or very stupid for saying, Yes, no problem, I will certainly care for your wolf-dog, to a woman whose children's names I do not even recall.

Before Chavez, I would make micro-promises to myself, micro-rewards I could receive if only I would leave the building. Fresh cigarettes, nice underwear, dark chocolate. I even wrote these items onto a list. Then I looked at my list. Was this World War

Two? With Grandmother drawing kohl lines up the backs of her legs and thickening the soup with a handful of mealy et cetera, et cetera . . . ? I made it a better list. I added to it soft cheese. Decent Calvados, if it could be located here. One very brave lipstick, red as Rosa Luxemburg. Mangoes. Pomelos. Anything you want, I told myself, because money is not the problem. It is not money or worry for the lack of money that has been keeping me from such things, only the process of getting to them. If I look up my account balance, I will see it is still loaded with all those insurance euros. (Not an act of God, apparently. Of anyone's God.) In the city so recently known as Home, Lotti has leased my apartment to a couple of architecture students from Norway, and their euros, too, pile up in my account. I am an imposter here, in this rabbity warren with its poor Marias, hiding behind a stranger's furniture, with a different stranger's dog. I simply arrived in this city and, like Chavez, curled into the smallest space I could find. And there is—for sometimes days, for sometimes whole weeks—no good thing I can dream up that will convince me to scurry out from it. No color of lipstick, no amount of fine stuff.

Why here? Because certain arrangements had already been set forth. Bruno, still engaged by an American institution, where he had accepted a yearlong appointment of hazy obligations, to shuffle his papers and to deliver the occasional rant on Metin Erksan or post-Fascist Cinecittà or whatever he was so inclined. Still at leisure to plot weekend indulgences of wineries and oyster farms and perhaps the five-hour odyssey to Westwood Memorial Park to stroll amidst the famous dead.

As long as I proceeded with the arrangements, he would

arrive in due course—sweating, overdressed, underpacked—already lighting up as he paid away the taxi driver, swearing that they had discovered their license at the bottom of a Bonux box.

Or, however he came: there he would be.

No matter that this American apartment—a furnished sublet acquired at short, disinterested notice—would not be to his satisfaction. A comfort to imagine him crowding its doorway, lighting up again despite building regulations, blowing disapproving smoke towards the broken light fixtures, the peeling paintwork, the bad art prints badly framed, the insufficient kitchen, before finally turning his longest-suffering face down to me:

Séverine, what have you got us into? You have a spider on your ceiling, or what?

Another reason: because here I was not known. Here no one thought to clutch my hands and wag their heads in tremendous pity. Another reason: the city so recently known as Home had become a facsimile of Home. Which was far more unsettling than being elsewhere. Each time I left or returned to the apartment I had shared with Bruno, there was still Christoph nodding gravely at the entrance of our building. At the MBA, still the exhibition of nineteenth-century figurative art. Outside the pharmacy, still the old Resistance fighter who would scream

Magdalena! for no reason. I should say, no reason anyone could determine. I am now ready to believe he had a reason. In any case. Past this man, forsythia was still blooming in the park, and Melancholy Vanessa still polished glasses at Les Pléiades, and the World Cup was still blaring from large screens, angled towards the entranceways of every other bar. As I have said, it was unnerving.

Disaster does not choose people. I try to console myself with this thought. Somebody must be standing on the bridge when it collapses, riding the plane when it goes down. Disaster does not care to seek us out; it simply is, and we are, and we meet along some terrible axis we are too small and too stupid to understand. I know, at the center of my logical self, that this is true. But at night it is not enough only to pull the curtains: I must also turn off all the lights and disconnect all the twinkling appliances and move around in the darkest dark so that nobody outside can know by my shadow exactly where I am, what I am doing. Even if what I am doing is only making tea, or giving water to the sick monstera plant. Once in bed I curl up into a ball, very tiny, so if someone were to enter my room I might be the very last thing they would notice.

I can get by on very little. All during my adult life I have been proud of this fact. I do not mean only food. A handful of sleep and a few pages of Saroyan. Black coffee and an eavesdropped conversation with a woman who claims to read the auras of birds. This is sufficient.

But what I was down to, what almost forced me out into the daylight was the fact that the only noncondiment items on my cupboard shelves were one jar of maraschino cherries and one half-bag of rice. And a jar of cherries is really perched upon the condiment/noncondiment divide. In the end I decided that I could last two days on that, perhaps three. Because there was still coffee, if half-stale, and also various spices to enliven the rice. And if one day I permitted myself a cigarette instead of lunch . . .

Oouut, bays Maria's poorly named dog.

And so it happens that I see my building from the outside for the first time in a week, and I am surprised to find it beautiful. It is, when one is looking from the street at its bricked-over carriageways and oriel windows.

Chavez walks as if he is performing dressage. He piaffes ahead of me at the end of his leash, stopping obediently when the crosswalk tells us *wait, wait, wait*, in a voice that sounds more forlorn with each repetition. *Wait, wait, wait*. But as soon as the traffic ceases we are parading again towards the water, and I remember—too late—that it is Sunday. Meaning: all of the people, all of their dogs. In this neighborhood the dogs all appear to be named for philosophers or jazz musicians or tragic figures from classic literature. We go past Mingus and Søren and Brutus, and whoever their people are. There are shouts for Gorky to come back right now, for Heisenberg to get out of that damn trash.

We are both slight women, myself and Maria. But the

difference is that I am not the one to be listened to, and Chavez leads me where he pleases. I am pulled like a clumsy musher in his wolfish wake, from hound to hound, fence post to light post, from cheerful Hello to How do. Does he like other dogs? these people ask. I say I do not know. Is he friendly with children? I say I do not know. What sort of breed is he? I pretend I have forgotten all of my English (except *I am sorry, I do not have much English*). We pass by one woman alone on a bench, who waves her magazine at us and calls to the dog by his name.

Chavez, beautiful beast, she says in a luxurious drawl, reaching lacquered nails to scratch his scruff. Who's your new mistress? Then she addresses me, winking, Where's the *old* mistress? Well, we all get traded in, eventually, don't we? Yes we do! Hahah!

I like the way she looks, this woman, with her gold-shadowed eyes and widely spaced teeth. As though she tried and failed at Hollywood in the seventies, but does not feel too bitter about it. I like her washed-up glamour. She reminds me of Lotti, I realize. But even so I do not wish to speak with her. It is difficult enough speaking with the real Lotti, who makes a point of observing, when she video-calls, how I have let the gray into my hair. (In fact, the gray has always been in my hair.) She is worried, I know, that I am fading away.

The woman on the bench says something additional to me in an odd relative of French that I am embarrassed not to understand. I nod and smile vigorously, agreeing to I do not know what, while tugging at the leash to dislodge Maria's dog.

No more, I tell Chavez once we are safely returned to the apartment. No more everybody-and-their-dog afternoons. Chavez does not bother to *Escóndete!* (perhaps my accent is not right?) but sits in the middle of the kitchen, one ear up, one ear down, as if to say, Woman who is not Maria, what is your problem?

But I remain firm. From now on, I inform him, we must be more strategic.

There is still, however, the supermarket to contend with—Maria's crumpled pair of twenty-dollar bills, paper-clipped together in a logic I do not comprehend, for the purchasing of Chavez's food.

A friend of mine did his dissertation on supermarkets. On the theories of supermarkets. Quoting heavily from fellow lunatics who had done the same. Meaning that for some years, this is all I heard about. To whom is this useful? I had wondered then. But now I am using it. For instance, I know the layout is far more complicated than simply: milk at the near end, bread at the far end, a vast territory of impulse purchases between. I understand that both the spacing of the aisles and the music overhead are working as allies to stall us. I am aware of which colors stimulate hunger, and which colors promise comfort, purity, vitality, robust familial relationships. All of this I can outfox to some success, breaking it down into harmless pieces. It simply takes some determination. The enemy is choice, or rather the appearance of choice—so it is a matter of restricting the influence of the appearance of choice. Simply, I will buy for myself only what is located between the entrance, the pet food aisle, and the checkout. A trajectory in the shape of an isosceles triangle. Having already excluded the possibility of bread and milk (except by accident) I feel more calm.

Once past the electronic doors, I look wistfully towards the bright pyramids of avocados and peaches in fresh produce. It is all right there, but in the wrong direction, and I march towards Aisle 9 and its seven-foot wall of dog faces, my mind buffered to everything but the brand Maria has written down for me. The dog on this package looks not the least bit like Chavez, but I collect two of each flavor and retrace my route back towards the checkout, tipping nonperishable items into my basket along the way. Oatmeal cookies. Cans of tomatoes and beans. Dried rigatoni. Whatever can be gleaned from the end-of-lane sale displays. Salt crackers. Make-believe orange juice. Sliced peaches. Thinking of bomb shelters, I assemble everything triumphantly upon the conveyor belt, and wait while the woman ahead of me interrogates her children about a pineapple.

Who put this thing in here? She lofts it up as though it might answer for itself.

Her children are silent. One chews his sleeve.

Well, sorry, guys, we're absolutely not taking this pineapple. Not after the lychee debacle.

The cashier places the pineapple in the corral for abandoned produce, and I avert my eyes so as not to show my elation. I stare hard into the label of the peaches—an orchard where a smiling bear pilots a tractor.

Once the woman ahead of me has paid and is shepherding her children towards the parking lot, I announce to the cashier that I will take the pineapple. As though I am the hero of the pineapple, when in fact I am already plotting to eviscerate it.

Be right with you, ma'am, says the cashier. Hey, Allen? Could you take this fucker back to produce? The pineapple is spirited away, and I watch mutely as my items follow each other over the scanner.

I remind myself that it is not even the best season for pineapples. Though in fact I do not know if this is so in this part of the world.

In the apartment, I place a bowl on the floor. I pour food into the bowl until it is full, Chavez eats the food until the bowl is empty, and this is satisfying in exactly the way watching animals eat is satisfying.

For myself I open the jar of peaches and arrange the slices on a plate in a spiral, as though this presentation means all the difference between meal and snack. I dust the peach slices with sumac and eat them with my fingers.

I am woken, this first night of dog-minding, by the restless clattering of Chavez's claws on the kitchen tiles. *Chit chit chit chit chit.* For a moment I think the frantic tapping is Bruno, bullying his typewriter as an ugly deadline rears up. He had twelve years on me, and was still in the habit of using the electric typewriter he had upgraded to—*upgraded to!*—in the eighties. It was not an elegant machine, but of course I could not bring myself to throw it away. Perhaps the fledgling architects are using it now.

I do not mind so much being woken. When I call to Chavez he comes, dropping down at the bedside with a dramatized *grouff.* I venture a hand from the covers to reassure him he belongs here, here for now, and fall asleep again holding on to an ear.

Our second walk proves more successful than the first. In the still-dark morning I take him out, when the gulls are scooping mollusks up from the lake and then flapping up and dropping them from great heights in order to smash them open. The wet clacking sound they make—are they clams? *Moules?*—when hitting the hard ground reminds me of a poem, but I do not remember whose, exactly. Only that it includes this English word, *clacking*, and was the first place I encountered it.

I watch the gulls so as not to watch Chavez, to save us both from embarrassment. When he is finished I pick up after him and we return home, creeping together past the doorways of our sleeping neighbors, the sound from his large feathery paws disappearing into the green hallway carpet.

We pass most of this day watching brief, grainy, unhappy footage on my laptop, and in the evening I type out an interview between an astronomer and a journalist who cannot quite manage to pronounce the name Churyumov-Gerasimenko.

Work still finds me through a little hole in the universe. The hole in question is my own name at gmail dot com. This reminds me sometimes of these—how are they called? These systems with the canisters of rolled-up documents which go whooshing along inside tubes? Over your head and through some secret arteries behind walls. Anyway. The work is transcribing faraway spoken interviews into neat scripts, sans disfluencies, in two or more colors. It arrives mostly from journalists. The journalists are mostly the old acquaintances of Bruno and myself. Their interviews are not always interesting. Often, these days, they are not interesting at all.

Not so long ago there were the occasional alarming subjects to reckon with. A man convicted of vampirism. A woman who had rented out her very young daughter to men in exchange for drug money. Sometimes I would need to remove my headphones and return to my desk with brandy in order to continue transcribing. But this work is all soft stuff now, all baby mush. Conversations with dreary economists and with people who have won things. Opinions of François Hollande's opinions on Fashion Week. No surprises, good or bad. *Give the poor woman something to think about*, I imagine them telling each other, all the way at the other end of this air tube (*pneumatique*, I just remembered). But of course, never *too* much to think about; nothing which might upset, invite dark thoughts, trigger, *déclencher.* As if I no longer have access to real-time news, to radios and televisions and papers, for instance the plane wreckage in the Ukrainian field of wheat and Queen Anne's lace. The first reports to emerge are lists of things: parking tickets, a scattered deck of cards, a child's book. Instead of bodies, we are shown the small strips of fabric wound around tree branches to flag where the bodies are.

In the end, though, we are still shown the bodies.

After transcribing the astronomer and the stumbling journalist, I type up a conversation with a children's author about an award she has just received. The book is said to have an environmental agenda. Otters in sweaters, I learn, can sell anything.

For walking Chavez, it is not so difficult to find unpeopled hours. These are the hours when I am most awake, in any case, when everybody else is not. And Chavez seems not to mind. We settle upon late nights and very early mornings, when there is still the glow of lights strung all the way around the lake—bright little stations we can move between. *Festooned* is the word. For lights like that. At these times there is occasionally the small matter of cats and Chavez wanting to eat them. But the squirrels are all curled away somewhere, so it is really an even trade, cats for squirrels. The lake bobs with ducks who are asleep, looking precisely like decoys out there with their heads tucked into their wings. The wind slowly spinning them around, as if they are as light as balsa. What bad could happen here?

There is a part of the self which is not yet caught up to the airplane age, part of the self which must journey as if by sea, while the rest of the body and brain and—soul? Fine, okay, I will say "soul"—might move at whatever absurd speeds we demand of them, at 500 knots amidst prepackaged meals and magazine advertisements for singing toothbrushes. Or perhaps it is precisely the soul that is so slow, that travels at such a lag. And so in my first weeks here I believe I weighed less—do you understand?—and I moved through these strange streets fearless even of the things

I knew to be afraid of: men who waited in parked cars nodding along to no radio, or the ones who squatted in doorways yelling disgusting things. News of gun-grazed innocents who were simply on their way to buy soda but were caught in crossfire. The statistics which Lotti helpfully sent to me: one robbery for every hundred residents, one car theft for every forty, and so on. These things did not register.

But soon enough the fear arrived, very sudden. It came right up and pounded me in a restaurant, a few bites into a harvest salad, and that was the last time I ate from other people's cutlery.

It was Bruno who coerced me into this habit in the first place, of eating out. Before him it seemed an extravagance to be doing so on ordinary days, for no special reason. But he was always given to extravagance.

I have said I can get by on little. Not so when I was young. When I was young I wanted to taste something from every plate. Again, I do not only mean food.

You'll spoil, my mother told me, and she did not mean only my appetite.

But my grandmother said this was the ideal way to go about life—by taking a little of all of it—and she seemed far happier than my mother, so I continued.

What changed? I am asking myself this only now. It could not have been just the one thing. It could not have been so simple as: I simply became less hungry. Or: I became content with what I had.

Hunger, for me, became Pavlovian. I imagine this is true for many. In recent years, it was the music of Oum Kalthoum which would cause me to be hungry. When not indulging in restaurants, Bruno liked to cook along to her mournful quarter-tone wavering. Dancing bearish but light-footed around our small kitchen, waking fennel and coriander seeds in spitting pools of ghee. Slathering aubergine with harissa and other strong spices he could detect over the taste of his constant cigarettes. So much garlic that I would be kept awake with the persistent ringing of it in my teeth and tongue. It was never enough for him to fill up a room with his voice and his opinions: he must overtake through every sensory means available.

After so many academics with beautiful hands who smelled like soap or nothing and made no sound when they climaxed, Bruno was like a motorcycle rally in all of his noise, all of his heat and smoke and vroom. He smelled as I imagined a seal might, like an oilskin jacket, only more so. It is hard to say why I liked this. It is hard to explain why I liked many things about him.

He was a lout and a drunk, no question. Perpetually in the process of sweating out a hangover, only to replenish it shortly after. One night I watched him drink a candle. It had lit us faithfully through aperitifs and dinner and was now lighting us through his demolition of a recent film by a much-lauded American director.

What do you say, Sévvy? Think these wankers believe they've created an "hommage" to Kaurismäki, or are they just hoping everybody somehow missed *Man Without a Past*? I am thinking my review will just be a list of ways I would like to strangle them. No reasonable person would stop me.

Then he reached for his whisky glass, but instead took a furious swig from the candle, filling his mouth with molten wax. Then bellowing and bellowing like a freight train, spitting half-solidified globs all over his plate of lemon tart.

Perhaps, when taken all together, it is obvious why I liked him. He was nothing like myself. I studied to be a journalist, but was too interrogative. One might think this is a good thing, but one would be mistaken. I was the wrong sort of interrogative, unraveling everything in my head until each question became a bundle of loose threads instead of a clean and shining dart. During the interviews I attempted, this bundle of loose threads would ignite into flames—*whoomph!*—and burn to nothing in a second. I would seize up entirely, having nothing left either to say or to ask. *Girl reporter*, some inner voice was always ready to condescend.

Bruno's questions were clear and direct, proper fléchette questions, and often he felt confident in answering them for himself.

What is this shit? This is Kieslowski for idiots, that's what it is.

How could anyone be so sure of anything? It was beyond me. I thought it very shortsighted—very male, in fact—to be so immune to the terrifying number of variables. But in the same instance it was comforting to be close to.

There is one particular lakeside place which Chavez especially enjoys to sniff around, where there are some viewfinders set on stands. These do not require any coins to look through, and are capable of being swung around 360 degrees to point at whatever one might want to see up close, though it is rare that I see anyone using them. Of course, it is rare that I see anyone at all, considering the hours of our expeditions, and this is the point.

Generally, I am content to look at whatever the last viewer was looking at. Generally, this is the building across the lake, which looms several stories above its neighbors in much Churrigueresque frosting. It looks as if it, too, is in exile, as if it has run away from Salamanca and is doing a not-so-good job of remaining inconspicuous. At the fourteenth floor there is a glass atrium which wraps around the building like a mantle and this is always lit, all through the night and darker mornings, though I never see any person standing up there. *Now*, I sometimes will through the binoculars. Be there *now*. But whoever might be up there never is.

Chavez goes about the methodical business of marking everything as his own. When I become disappointed by the building, I search instead for the fleet of pelicans, who move in unison and fish in perfect synchrony, as if they are of clockwork. I imagine beneath the water some interconnected means of propulsion, some shared system of cranks and gears. But I have seen them lift into the air before, separate after all. The orchestration, how they plunge their necks beneath the surface all at once; there must be some purpose for it. It must dazzle the fish.

Inside the apartment, I free Chavez from his leash in time to catch my laptop ringing. Lotti, the screen tells me. I accept, voice only—since the recent comments about my disheveled appearance, my gamine-style dress, I have pretended my camera is broken. Really it is just stuck over with something that I stuck there myself.

It is more than my appearance, if I am honest: it is hers, unchanged, and the appearance of my old life there in her background, also unchanged. The view from her window the same as the view I shared with Bruno, though from a slightly different altitude, incorporating a little more sky; we lived two floors below.

Sévvy? Oh good, I called and called. Debbie Harry wants to say hello—say hello, Debbie Harry—and that she doesn't want you cavorting with any new cats.

I have not mentioned Chavez. I think back to the woman on the bench—Lake Lotti, Lotti of the Lake, with the gold-shadowed eyes—and have the cuckoo thought that she might have passed along this information, about my caring for Chavez. (And its reverse—that she perhaps knows the things Lotti knows.)

We're not allowed pets in this place, is the only not-crazy thing I find to say aloud.

Savages, says Lotti. I almost hear her satisfied frowning.

Chavez puts his muzzle into his empty food bowl and scrapes it across the floor towards me with a low, imploring groan.

What's going on back there?

Water heater, I lie, stopping the bowl under my shoe.

That reminds me, Lotti says. The architecture students? They have been complaining of a draft. Should I send Ramon? Ramon is so expensive, I know, but reliable. Also, the students have rigged up a few things. Shelves, and some kind of system for a projector, which I don't think can be removed without some harm to the plaster . . .

I tell her that the plaster does not matter. I tell her, please send Ramon, that I will pay Ramon, and that she is a saint for seeing to all this. Then I hastily say goodbye before we can talk about the reason the old apartment is sheltering architecture students, before the conversation can turn Bruno-ward. After closing the laptop I gently reprimand Chavez for his noise, though in truth I am growing to be fond of his noise.

I was once a great lover of silence, certain silences. In the time when silences were still promises. A *hush*, I suppose, is the better word for what I loved—a quietness that looks forward to a particular moment but is in no particular hurry to get there.

Hushes I loved in my old life: during concerts, the hush between the final note and the lowered violin; between the lowered violin and the applause. Between the words of slow, thoughtful speakers. Art galleries in the low season. Snow-filled avenues before the plows swept in. The sweet, confined hush of a long car journey, after one passenger has fallen asleep. Really I mean Bruno; that passenger, those hushes. For the little adventure he was insistent to have, I drove him as far as Paris, from where he would fly. Couriering him like a package, he joked, in the big old boat of a car which I enjoyed far too much to trade it for something more economical, more svelte. Bruno teased me for this environmental atrocity, but he loved this ridiculous car also. Of course he did—it was huge and hungry and it ate up the road like a monster, and aside from him, it was the most ostentatious thing I had to show for myself.

Between Beaune and Nitry he slept and there was hush, magnificent hush, and then he woke and we argued. Stupid, I said. Arrogant. This *Boys' Own* adventure.

It will be a little guided, as I have already explained, he attempted to reassure me.

A *little* guided? I repeated, unsure whether he was playing things down or up, whether it was not guided at all, or if it was in fact the Contiki tour of civil unrest.

This guide of his was the brother of an old friend from Ankara, who was now writing articles for an independent paper, published across the border and smuggled in weekly, depending on how safe were the roads. Which sounded to me worse than no guide.

Why, I demanded, knowing I had already lost, but not content to do so spinelessly. Was he aware that he was not himself a documentarian? That he was merely qualified for talking about the works of other documentarians?

He sat there silent for once, petulant, hating me to say this but knowing it was true.

You just enjoy taking pictures, I went on. Also you think

you are immune to many real and terrible things. Cirrhosis of the liver, for instance, and bad credit ratings, and now war.

You are overreacting, he said. It'll be a . . . These things happen everywhere. Why leave the house? Might get flattened by a bus. You know the first civilian deaths in any war are those who stand staring mousishly out of their own front doorways? Look it up if you don't believe, Séverine.

But he was telling me this only because it had already been arranged, and flights had been confirmed, and there was nothing in the world I could say which would convince him to cancel plane tickets.

I remember we stayed overnight in the Hotel Gabriel. We repaired in its lounge, over a bottle of Roussanne. That night we were like new with each other, while at the same time being like two very old people. As if we had snuck away together from the nursing-home prom. We lay there whispering, scheming. What we would do when he returned. A holiday to Lake Bethmale. Bethmale was the lake into which we threw our engagement rings when we decided not to get married (though in the end, we married anyway).

I was his second wife, his young wife.

Young enough to still have blemishes, I see, his first wife observed in a letter I should not have read.

I was thirty-four then. (Not so very young, I had thought, though later I would find cause to revise this.)

What she was implying, I think, was: young enough to still have children.

But there wasn't a child. There was almost a child. There was an almost-child. There was a child, and she almost made it. It has been several years, and there are at once too many and not enough ways to say this.

When Bruno came into the hospital I put my hand up to his sagging face.

They're going to boot me out of the Young Wives' Club for this, I tried to joke, and he tried to laugh.

No no no, they'd never. They'd never ever—they'd be lost without your unmatched macramé skills.

But his face had refused to hold the laugh, and he leaned down and sobbed openly into my hair.

I still have the stretchmarks she gave me. Something. For some years afterwards, I imagined these marks were encrypted, that there was something I could have done differently or better if I had only understood and deciphered in time. Often, when making love, I would try to hide them with darkness or with sheets, covering up the way my body had failed me, or I had failed my body. But in the hotel, for whatever reason, I allowed them to be seen, to be traced by his thick fingers.

In the morning tenderness lingered around the margins of a hasty continental breakfast and the madness of Charles de Gaulle. Bruno proceeded on to Istanbul to meet his connection, and I drove alone back to Lyon. Back to the apartment, where Debbie Harry had discovered and emptied all her little cachettes of food, and had also destroyed a few books in retribution for being left behind. Her tiny needle fangs had found their way into some slim volumes from the lower shelf, books I had read in school. I picked up a ravaged edition of Colette (you are being ironic? I asked regarding the teeth marks) and took both destroyer and destroyed to bed. The drive and fending off worry for Bruno had exhausted me, and I read the same line several times before falling asleep with the lamp on.

I realize I am still scuffing about in the slippers from the Hotel Gabriel. They were intended as disposable, and still I kept them, and brought them over here. Even though I brought so little. I am being sentimental, I know. Sentimental and unhygienic: the soles of these slippers have become very grimy, squashed flat from so many months wedged under my feet. The hotel insignia, once gold, is now the dirty yellow of dried mustard. I must throw them out and buy new ones. I will. Fresh slippers will go on the list. But really I know this will not happen.

How did those first days pass, in the sudden vacuum caused by the absence of Bruno? I padded about the apartment noiselessly in my hotel slippers (then clean). I fell back into my meeker, meager ways. Even the music I chose to play was without words. I took some guilty pleasure from the quiet, but I kept my phone close by to receive messages. He had arrived safely with Ozgur in Gaziantep. They were consuming much arak. Could I please return his borrowed films to the library, as he was receiving angry emails.

The situation was not so dire then as now. Or, we did not

know it to be. Homs did not yet look like World War Two Warsaw. Or, there had not yet been published the photographs which showed Homs to look like World War Two Warsaw. I worried, yes. But not so terribly, if I am honest.

Then nothing for several days. And nothing for several more, the hush soured to an awful silence. The loudest silence of our lives, Lotti's and mine. A week into this silence, Lotti brought her things down from her own apartment to make camp on our couch, so that any news might find the two of us simultaneously. At intervals our phones skittered across the kitchen table, propelled by messages of support from friends. Everyone reverently spelling their words in full, restricting emoji content to cartoon hearts and candles. *Stay strong. There is still hope.* The messages would cease for a few hours overnight, then resume each morning as people were waking, pausing between bites of breakfast or while waiting for the iron to heat up for their work clothes. Our refrigerator became a miniature container yard filled with bright plastic tubs, meals prepared by neighbors and left discreetly in the hallway outside the door, while inside Lotti and myself filled several ashtrays, brewed a dozen cafetières of strong coffee, and sat up collaborating on our *please don'ts* and our *have mercies* in case the media people might want to broadcast them.

To whom would they be broadcast? Of whom were we pleading mercy? We did not know. There had not yet been any demands, for any things. No demands even for the absence of things: air strikes, sanctions, certain prisoners detained in certain facilities.

Still we devoted ourselves unreservedly to this pretense of agency. To the fantasy of choice—which words might be the right words. We drank more coffee and read over our appeals gritty-eyed, waiting for the arrival of stipulations that might render them (and ourselves) useful.

When at last the phone rang, and I answered to a stranger's voice, the demand was only for dental records.

These I could have provided from memory:

Dead upper left incisor. Killed in the line of duty, Bruno would boast. A swift *coup bas* outside of a nightclub in the Eighteenth. Delivered by a novice director whose debut Bruno had dismissed as flaccid.

Second lower-right premolar, cracked on an olive pit during a short holiday in Figueres. A split that ran right down below the gum line. This was met with surprisingly good humor, given it was from a Castelvetrano, beloved. Bruno had merely tongued the broken tooth, murmuring that they had brought so much pleasure over the years, he'd be a monster to complain now, and continued through the meal with unfamiliar delicacy.

A solitary remaining wisdom tooth, lower left, rotated 25 degrees counterclockwise. The other three had been pulled decades earlier. This one held on, but woefully, intermittently giving him trouble.

It's pining, he said when it ached. Thinks itself the last of its tribe, poor brute. Better kiss me to make it shut up.

———

Yes, I explained such things aloud, if you can believe, if in not quite so many words. As long as I was speaking they would not be able to elaborate on this need for dental records. Lotti, who had been balled up a long time on the couch, not-sleeping, lifted her head and looked at me, dazed. Me, who sounded deranged, I realized in that moment.

A cough from the detective on the other end of the line.

Madame . . .

Yes, I conceded. Dental records. And hung up to go and search for them.

Very early one morning I wake from an unpleasant dream, or rather a dream so unreachably pleasant it is unbearable: The phone rings. Yes. Yes, we can meet at Bethmale. I can make all the arrangements. I just have to repair this broken stereoscope.

Sleep, in some ways, is worse than supermarkets, because I do not know who or what manufactures this experience, or precisely what it is that they want of us.

I feel with my feet for slippers, finding fur instead of toweling, along with a grunt. Chavez is already there, waiting. I must have been talking in my sleep.

What highly confidential information did I reveal? I ask him.

Ouut, he answers, changing the subject.

Out, it is raining. It has been raining steadily and patiently for some days, and so to save the floors I secure plastic sandwich bags around Chavez's feet in the way I have seen on certain other dogs. He acquiesces to this indignity. I acquiesce to stand with him in the downpour, the streetlight seeping into the wet air, the dark lake applauding. The birds are all elsewhere. Hurry up, I think to Chavez, but he persists to pee on everything, even though the weather makes this futile.

It is this time that I see for once, looking through the binoculars as rain needles the lake, people on the fourteenth floor of the exiled building. And upon seeing them, I must immediately look away. It is nothing sinister I catch them at, nothing that embarrasses. Just ordinary living that they are displaying up there. A couple, not young. A white-haired man standing the way one stands to watch television news. A slight woman in a blue shirtdress moving back and forth across the room, in and out of frame, as if everything were normal. How is it they cannot know they are so visible? They must know. And so I wonder how it is they can stand it.

Rain hammers my cheap pharmacy umbrella, as though it has come with urgent news. I pull the leash to dissuade Chavez from some smell he has been captured by, feeling curdled and ill, and we turn for home.

At the crosswalk—*wait, wait, wait*—a chubby girl wearing a transparent raincoat over miniature shorts bops her ample behind to music leaking from her headphones, and I feel irritation and then dismay—am I joyless?

How? They would not tell me how, or could not. Not for certain. Maybe strangled, maybe shot, or stabbed, quite possibly macheted. But then burned. Beyond recognition. And the car he was in. Almost beyond recognition. It had once been a Subaru, and it was rented from the airport. The former Subaru was found on the safe side of the border. The safe side of the border. The safe side of the Turkish border deep in a Turkish forest. They made him drive it there. Not Bruno—the Ankaran friend's brother, he was driving. Bruno was only the passenger.

He was only, he was only. As though it matters.

Was it random or specific? They couldn't tell that, either. Valuable things ignored—his watch, phone, et cetera—ruled out simple robbery. There were suspicions but no evidence. Just as likely a crazed loner as any of the other, more infamous possibilities.

How? I still want to know. Notwithstanding who. If there was footage, I would have watched it. Many times, I would have watched, I know. I would not have been able to stop myself. Instead, I have watched all the other footage. Scrolled and played and replayed. And when there is new footage that bubbles up from the dark belly of the internet, I watch it also. This, too, is something I cannot help. So much for the protective efforts of my colleagues.

*

The day upon which Maria is supposed to come and collect Chavez arrives and disappears like the TGV through an insignificant town. Then the morning after this, and the one which follows do not bring her. I call the number she has left for me to call if something happens to Chavez or the building burns down or some other catastrophe occurs, but the numbers do not reach to anywhere or anyone, just the apology of a robot voice explaining that nobody is at the end of this sequence of numbers.

I am not sure if it is my position to do something now, to call and make some report or other. For the first time, I properly worry—how bad was this bad husband of Maria's? I worry also whether they confiscate the dogs of missing persons. This is unlikely, but just in case, I decide I will not mention Chavez when calling authorities. However, the weeks vanish without me calling any authorities.

During this time, the only mail which arrives for Maria is in the form of bills, threats of disconnections, and finally notices of disconnections. There is also one subscription to a Spanish science magazine, in which I appreciate some of the graphs and diagrams. Aside from this there is nothing but junk.

I try to interpret if Chavez is concerned for her, whether he is pining. One night we climb up to Maria's apartment together, and he circles the main room and sniffs everything to make sure it still belongs to him, and then huffs down onto the woven rag rug in the center of the room in a way that seems *abattu*. Chavez, I mean, though the rug seems despondent also. But when I go to the door the dog follows without protest. We return downstairs, where he settles down Sphinx-like beside me as I pull my laptop onto my knees and begin a new search for the videos I know I should not be searching for.

In the footages that do not show Bruno, the hostages appear shaken and malnourished. Or else they appear sinewy and stoic. They have not had any alcohol in many months, this can be seen in comparing the footage to the photographs from fishing trips and honeymoons and family holidays that are published by less morbid media. Their clothes are sandblasted to no color, or rotting away with a greenish damp. On occasion their skin, along with their expressions, have taken on some elemental likeness—stone, or earth, or closely grained wood—as if to chameleon to their particular surrounds, or to separate themselves completely from undependable flesh and blood.

They deliver, sometimes, rehearsed statements to families and governments. Sometimes these include appeals, demands, bargains, and then the footage is over, the screen blacks out harmlessly.

Other times, no bargains are to be offered, and what follows was always going to follow, was always crouching there, hidden in plain silence at the end of the statement.

I smooth down the ears of Chavez. Does he know that what he sees is terrible? I think yes. I suspect he is this smart, and because of this I feel some guilt to be exposing him to these scenes. It is not so good for him, I think, to watch these things only. And so I play sometimes the absurd English comedy shows Bruno enjoyed, and which I could apparently never appreciate the genius hilarity of. It is a parrot in a tuxedo, or whatever, I would say. It is a man walking idiotically—so what? And this, where people are attempting to remain in hiding, behind bushes and trees and cars, but each time the hiding place is exploded. I still do not see where it is so funny.

Towards Christmas I am taking downstairs the small amount of rubbish which Chavez and I succeed to make between us during a week. Mostly it is hair: my dark-with-gray hair, his white hair. Enough to construct another Séverine and one other Chavez, almost. I notice that huddled around the dumpster are some of Maria's possessions, packed into cardboard boxes. I determine they are Maria's by the old stack of *Muy Interesante*. Inside the dumpster there are larger items; chairs and clotheshorses, the despondent rug. I place my rubbish bag onto the ground and go to the front of the building. The name next to the buzzer for Maria's apartment still reads Quintana. But the name next to the buzzer for my apartment still reads Schutt, and that is not my name. Though it possibly could be, I sometimes think. The only real mail which ever arrived at this apartment was one letter for Ms. A. Schutt, which I marked for return and sent away. *Avis. Anne. Arlene. Arabella. Alma.* Nothing addressed to her has arrived since. I could be Ava Schutt—there is no one to say otherwise.

I return to search amongst the boxes, and find the photographs of the daughter and son of Maria. They are there amongst the paper flowers and the god's-eyes made in blue and yellow yarn wound around crossed popsicle sticks, jumbled in with clothes and tangled strings of colored lights. Everything that was upstairs is now downstairs; plates painted in crimson and peacock, Maria's bright scarves and tiny fierce shoes. An ugly winter coat which I am unable to picture her in, because it was not yet winter when she left. There are some toy animals belonging either to Chavez or the children. I pick up one small felt walrus and turn him over to assess if he has been assaulted by tooth marks or dog spit. He fits into my pocket. I try to imagine what Maria will want most when she returns, and I transfer these things into one box: a spiral notebook of handwritten recipes, one silver pashmina, along with the photographs and postcards and children's crafts. I realize I do not know Maria well enough to know what she would most want, so I make one more box full of things I would want, and I carry both upstairs to store inside my closet. That is all there is room for. But then I go down and carry back one last box, made heavy by dinnerware, dollar votive candles, and cloth-bound novels in Spanish. My apartment becomes full of Maria Quintana's apartment. When I offer Chavez the walrus, he accepts it as delicately as if it is a Communion wafer, then shakes his head violently to murder it.

In the few cold weeks that barely amount to winter, Chavez and I follow the sunlight around the apartment. The monstera plant recovers. Encouraged, I commit to more plants—midget magnolia, purple jade, elephant food. Chavez ruins the ones he does not care for. Or perhaps he ruins the ones he cares for too much—this issue of translation persists. In any case, he is indifferent to the succulents, and so they flourish.

The world trickles back to me, slowly, percolated through headphones, in many voices: *Nothing left, for food. In the last days we eat even the toothpaste. I think: someone comes soon. Someone must. But no one comes. When she stops breathing, I breathe to her. For how long I don't know. Many hours. Because what if help comes just around that corner? I keep breathing to her. I refuse to believe it is too late until it is a long way past too late.*

Once more I am to be trusted with the hearing of such recollections; reports of wars, diseases, cruelties. Terrible things recounted by unfamiliar voices who nevertheless manage to continue broadcasting from the mouths of storekeepers, cleaning staff, people passed in the street, as gradually Chavez and I take our walks later and later in the mornings, earlier and earlier in the nights. In fact this is only the illusion, of earlier and later: it is simply the fact of winter leaning quietly towards spring, the light stretching out across the length of a day, infiltrating our routine. The sensation is of the world gaining volume, the little metallic light stealing in at the edges of sky, skin and fur taking on an icy, drowned color. We abandon the hours of dogs and wolves for the hours of Tai Chi seniors and yoga boot camps and seagull feeders. The hours of boom boxes and picnic rugs, hazy ukulele circles, after-school gymnastics troupes.

One afternoon a postcard appears in my mailbox, an Anywhere image of a beach and palm trees.

Querida S, I read while standing at the box, then hurry upstairs to place it written-side down on the table, afraid of what it will go on to say. I am embarrassed to admit that I leave it there overnight, offering the words underneath a chance to kindly rearrange or erase themselves, to scuttle away like beetles, the way they sometimes will in dreams. When I have finally collected enough courage, I find that what it says is nothing much.

Dear S. Very peacefully here, but have some pain for (smudge) to not come back these days. I think to you often. Thank you always for your kind. M.

I am at the same time relieved and offended on the behalf of Chavez. But one's dog is not one's children, I understand. I expect another card but there is never another. Or if there is, it does not reach me.

Summer arrives. In March, taking everyone by surprise. Chavez suffers the entrapment of his thick fur, seeking the cool kitchen tiles, the bathtub, finally settling to stretch out beneath my desk with his head resting on a ziplock bag of frozen grapes, while I attempt to work. Now and again I stray to browsing international quarantine laws. *Cargo*. It is not a very comfortable word. He does not take up so much space, really. Even when complaining.

On one of these false summer nights, I am woken from the darkest parts of sleep to find Chavez, crouched before the apartment's door, his snout pushed to the sill, teeth bared at whatever might be outside in the hallway. I lower myself to the floor alongside him, smelling dog breath and an unfamiliar, angry rank. Burying my hands into the dog's ruff makes him quiet, only; his fur remains bristled, his ears high and sharp, on radar. I listen for human movements—any movements—on the other side of the door. The thin wedge of light that intrudes underneath is not broken by any shadow. There is nothing. Or if there is something, it is very small, a rat or escaped hamster, or it has already moved on. I coax Chavez away before blocking the offending light with a bath towel rolled into a snake. That is that. Though I wake soon after to Chavez patrolling the room, back and forth, back and forth, tossing his great head and pawing and whimpering into corners. It is a noise, I determine, a dog-maddening sound pitched beyond my simple hearing. Or else it is a gas leak, or something living in the walls.

Or, I have damaged him, after all, with my gloomy obsessions.

Finally I convince him to be still. Summoning him up onto the bed, and pushing my toes into his fur in the way we have both come to appreciate: *I am here; I am here, also.* But each time I open my eyes I see the glint of his, watchful, in the dark.

Shortly before dawn, the building heaves. A shallow dream in which I missed a stair. Chavez is already awake—has perhaps been awake this whole while—sitting sentinel, looking impatient.

A second shudder passes through the building. (Yes, all right, I admit to him. I see now.) Something heavy thuds onto the floor of upstairs. A bad art print crashes from the wall, and from the kitchen comes the silvery sound of glassware turning to smithereens.

I take Chavez by the collar, unsure of where is the better place to be: doorway or bathtub or under a table, or whether it is best of all to run out into the open street. (*Disaster does not choose.*) Doorway, I decide. I hold to Chavez as we wait for whatever underlying forces to shift again, or cease shifting, while unnumbered feet pound along the hallway towards the exits.

We sit eye to eye, dog and I, until the stomping and the shouting has gone away, gone out. We stay like this, listening as the building settles with a harmless ticking, like the cooling sounds of a big machine.

Then the fire alarm begins its caterwaul, as if upholding appearances: a child who has fallen and takes a moment to decide that yes, this is an applicable moment to wail. Chavez howls in response, and the sprinkler system follows, raining upon the subleased furniture, upon the fallen art print, and all the boxes of rescued things that Maria will never, I know, be returning for.

Okay, I say, Uncle.

Out in the street, our neighbors have converged, in shoes and out of shoes, clutching children or animals or laptops, occasionally managing all three. The more organized have evidently studied quake preparedness, and are handing out from a bulk box of pharmacy protein bars, determined on maintaining energy levels, though it has only been twenty minutes.

The surrounding hills blink quietly with lights, showing no signs of unrest. Overhead, the power lines are slack and unsparking. Two boys, bored with waiting, have decided to document the almost-disaster on cell phone. We must look the most miserable, Chavez and myself, the most tragedy-struck; the last to emerge, the only ones drenched. The boys invent a more stirring narrative of our plight—*and this trained wolf dragged this woman to safety*—before turning the camera back towards our building, shaking the device for effect.

I imagine this footage finding its way, somehow, to Lotti, during her rigorous tallying of this country's perils.

Fault lines! she will call to say triumphantly. Did I not warn you? Though, in fact, fault lines had not featured in her catalog of menace.

As light comes into the sky I make out the small particulars of these faces around us, familiar and otherwise, and in some I read what I first believe to be grief, the shadow of possible loss. Then I understand that it is in fact not grief, but disappointment: they have done everything right. They have drilled and drilled, they have performed perfectly, but this is not the big one. This is only another drill. The big one is still to come.

The bells of Our Lady ring out across the lake, mournful and extravagant, though it is too early for any service. The street slowly empties of people, as if the signal has been issued that all is safe, now, that all may return to their homes.

———

In the city so recently known as Home, it will be 3:51 p.m., CET. Sunday. Winter will still be itself there, and Lotti will be pattering around her kitchen above the heads of the Norwegian architects, preparing for dinner. Perhaps making mercimek köftesi in the way their mother taught to her and Bruno. Her jewelry held aside in an empty wineglass so she can compress the lentil mixture very tightly between cupped palms. The art to it, Bruno insisted, his hands around my own, is pressing tight enough to leave an impression of one's lifeline. There.

The Once-Drowned Man

The once-drowned man hailed me from outside the county courthouse. He was trailing a little blue-and-leather suitcase. I figured it held legal documents or some such, but the fact was I saw him standing there at 2 a.m., and although he wore a suit he did not strike me as the solicitorial type. The suit was very nicely cut, though even I could tell it was a decade outdated. And also a little disheveled, with the shirt open at the collar. A button was off. I wondered whether he might have been the defendant in an important case that day, and spent some hours trying to console himself in some rat-nest or other. But his breath did not smell of drinking.

At first he only wanted to go as far as Lloyd's, pick up a few things, use the phone. Lloyd's then bed, he told me. I left the meter running. Then while he was in there he changed his mind. He came back out through the colored plastic streamers with a six-pack of seltzer and a potted baby spruce. The spruce was dressed for Christmas, but it was only October. When he climbed back into my cab, it was right into the passenger seat. Usually only the very old or the very tall did this. He settled the suitcase between his feet and the baby spruce between his knees. Then he turned to me, eyes crackling with an indistinct glory, a light that was infectious if perhaps not thoroughly sound.

He started: I try to honor every coincidence, you understand. (Here he put his hand on my shoulder. I looked at the hand. He took the hand away and continued.) This was meant to be an auspicious day for me. I still hope I might recover it. I have at least one sturdy friend in Canada, he said, though this friend seems no longer in the habit of picking up the phone. Doesn't this seem a fine night for it, though?

For what?

For Canada. It's only a squeak past the border, St. Kitts.

Tonight, I said. You mean this morning.

This very morning.

This very morning. I think that would make for an expensive coincidence.

We were one of only two cars in the lot. I tried to see through the windows of Lloyd's, whether my fare had knocked somebody down, or been the cause of some other commotion. But all appeared normal.

In any case, I said. I can't drive you across the border.

You ever tried? he asked. It against the law?

Probably it's against the law, I don't know. In any case. I won't get a fare back from way up there.

Of course I will pay your fare back. I've already factored that into the expense.

Also, I said, I am not carrying my passport.

Well, we can make a detour for your passport. We can factor that into expenses too.

I told him that would make a very long detour for us both.

He seemed to understand. He stroked the little spruce in thought, as if it were substitute for a beard. Okay, he said. Say you drive me to the border—am I then within my legal rights to walk over on my own two feet?

I'm sure that's allowed. But I don't make the rules.

Mother Maria, what fuss. In California, you wanna go to Mexico? You can just walk behind the fried chicken place and there it is: Bienvenido! A twelve-year-old with a gun who just nods at you. Bienvenido!

The airport would be cheaper, I offered. Cheaper and faster. Bet there's a dozen flights going up there come 6 a.m., I said, though in fact I had no idea.

You don't heed the news? he said. Could you look at my face, please. (I looked at his face.) Who with this face can trouble with airports nowadays? And fact is I never fly when I can help it. Especially never east. Flying against time—crazy. West isn't so bad. You only fly west, and you're ahead on time. Your whole life could be one long stretch of daylight. Look, all right, I know it doesn't exactly work that way, but you try explaining to me why not.

But I was too tired to explain to him why not. There's a train too, I said feebly. A train goes every day.

The trains are presently on strike, he said.

I had no answer for that. It was not known to me, whether or not the trains were on strike.

A woman's face appeared at the passenger window. She tapped on the glass with fake-jeweled fingernails. My fare waved at the running meter and shooed her away before I could intervene.

Forget the train, he said to me. Forget the airport. It has to be now, while I've got the Amplitude. The once-drowned man closed his eyes in burdened patience. Why are you trying to throw away a lucrative fare? You have kids to pick up?

No.

You got a man who's going to give you some trouble if you don't come home in time to make him breakfast?

I knew the sensible answer to this was yes. I told him no.

I make you nervous, that it?

No, I said, and this was a half-truth. My mother drove cabs. She kept a gun bulldog-clipped under the driver's seat. This in a country where people were less in the habit of shooting each other.

My fare shook his head. You don't think I'm good for it, he said. Listen, I believe in good faith. I live in accordance with those words—*In. Good. Faith*—but I appreciate that not everyone can afford to operate on the same principles. Hard times breed hard feelings. Tell me, how many miles is it, here to there?

I said I guessed it as three fifty.

The man fished a bill clip from an inside pocket of the shabby jacket. Three fifty, he repeated. So as a show of good faith, I am going to advance you for two hundred miles. That's about what I have on my person. In five hours the banks will open, and we'll settle up for the rest. Plus the same again for your return, word of honor.

The banks. What's wrong with an ATM?

A what?

You don't have a bank card? Plastic?

He gave me a wounded look. The world doesn't run on plastic, he said. It runs on paper. Paper and gasoline. He riffled all the larger bills out of his wallet, folded them over, and held them out.

I opened the bills, counted through them. He twisted the cap off a seltzer and put the bottle to his lips, taking a deep, doleful swallow as if to dissociate with my visible lack of good faith. Canada was at best four and a half hours beyond my designated radius, and Silas would not have been happy about his cab going so far without him. And I would not have wanted to ask Silas in the first place, because he would have said absolutely no, or else he'd have taken the ride over himself (all the long jobs were his, the fares to JFK and such). I was supposed to have the cab back in his driveway by quarter of three the coming afternoon. Clean, topped up with gas, with his take already calculated. Silas was not a man of faith as far as I knew, but there was a miniature bearded saint suction-cupped to the dashboard. Old plastic turned the color of a bad tooth. I wasn't sure which saint it was meant to be. It was possible Silas had simply chosen one in his own likeness, in an attempt to spook me honest.

What I'm saying is: I suppose I must have needed the money. Of course I needed the money. People who do not need money do not drive cabs, no matter what they'll tell you. More than likely I'd already spent the money, in one way or another, and now owed it to telephone and electricity companies, to banks and pawnbrokers and landlords.

I folded up the bills and tucked them away.

I'll stop into a brick-and-mortar for the rest, he promised again. Soon as they open, first thing. That's just what I have right now on my person, excepting some smalls and coinage for food. But you can hold on to my license and passport as collateral, if you like. There's even my birth certificate here somewhere, he said, hunting through the suitcase, then his pockets.

He offered all this with an expression of guilelessness, his face open as a baby's. In all good faith, I am sure, that I would wave this gesture away. As if there was anything to stop him recovering these after my body had been ditched.

My passport is not in my birth name, as you will likely observe, he said, and as such it is additionally precious to me.

Here it is, I thought. The booklet he'd produced looked very crisp, freshly minted.

Where has it been, I asked. I mean, what stamps does it have?

He took the document back and flipped through it. Charles de Gaulle, he read. Heathrow. Harmless places.

But you should rough it up a little bit. It looks untraveled. In my opinion.

He held the passport out the window and tipped a little seltzer on it, shook it in the wind.

Of course I had my doubts. But by this stage I had already spent the money, at least in my mind. And I had already made peace with Silas, also in my mind. A full week's takings in six hours. Twelve hours if you counted the way back, but I'd do those hours with the radio up and maybe a bottle of Fernet Branca for mouthwash, and the small luxury of my own thoughts.

All right, I said. Which crossing?

The Falls. Over the Rainbow Bridge.

It sounds like dying, I said, keying the ignition.

Hear hear, he said.

Once we got onto the 90, the once-drowned man let out a long breath I wasn't aware he'd been holding. He rubbed his palms into eyes leaded by decades of bad sleep. Then he rolled down the window and breathed some more.

This is fine air, isn't it? And this is a nice, nice thing you're doing for me, he said. You want to know the nicest thing anybody's said to me in I don't know how long? The dentist told me I have an uncomplicated mouth. And he didn't even mean that stuff wasn't going wrong in there, just that whatever was wrong was fairly garden-variety stuff. That's the nicest thing in I don't know how long. And however uncomplicated it was, it still hurt like all hell, let me tell you. Makes me tired. What about you, what're you tired of?

And I knew well enough that it was just anxious talk, conversational caulk, but there was so much highway between here and Canada, and while I hoped he'd eventually drop off into sleep and stay dropped off for most of it, I figured it couldn't hurt to give him a real answer. I wanted easy feelings for the waking hours. We were only just past the bedroom communities to the bedroom communities—I don't know if there's a better name for those, but they make me uneasy. So I said, This. These places make me tired.

These places, he said, looking out the window at the corrugated cement noise barriers. These places don't even exist.

I kept thinking on it, what else tired me. Fares offering me drugs instead of money. Fares offering me sex instead of money. Fares acting like fares instead of people, making me think of people as fares. Fares who asked me to drive them way out to those box-store outlets and had me wait in the parking lot while they bought build-it-yourself bunk beds and four-gallon jugs of fake syrup. Speaking in gallons, that tired me too. Ounces and yards and miles. The entire imperial system. Fares trying to guess where I was from and guessing wrong, always. Sometimes I said yes to places I'd never set a foot in, just so I didn't have to listen to a stranger tell me what they thought they knew about my actual home country—another thing that caused my mind to drift into the growlers.

Did I say these things aloud? I suppose I must have, because a little farther along the once-drowned man surprised me by guessing my home correctly. No one ever had before. I didn't spring to either confirm or deny, and he didn't try to tell me what he knew about the place. But the air in the cab felt slightly charged after this, as though he'd said *Rumpelstiltskin*.

You don't have much of an accent, he said.

I wouldn't know, I said.

I have forgotten the language in which my parents spoke to me as a child, he said. The language in which I learned to count, and tell time. How is this possible? When I have sufficiency in so many other languages now.

He reached forward to touch the saint on the dashboard, but did not touch. You're Catholic, he said.

It isn't mine, I told him.

As for myself, I have had the Catholic beaten into and beaten out of me at various intervals. I'm a nullifidian now. You've heard of Kateri Tekakwitha?

Somewhere, I said.

There was a sign just now, he said. Some way up ahead we'll pass her shrine. Patron of exiles, of émigrés. Lily of the Mohawks. Know what her first miracle was? Turning smooth and white after death. They'll try and canonize you just for that. They'll make a smooth white marble statue of you and set it out alone in the forest. Sounds lonely, does it not? I visited her once. Birds had come and nested on her breast. Here, he said, patting his shirt pocket. Like a sacred heart made of mud and sticks and regurgitated bird stuff. Blessed Kateri. I bet those birds were migratory.

The émigré has many saints, I wanted to say, but I was afraid he'd want the list.

Katherine, he went on, reading from my ID card. Katherine with a K. That a popular name where you're from?

I shrugged. It's popular here. It's always dangling there, in the ready-made souvenirs, fridge magnets and so on.

I told him that I hoped my name (in fact chosen from a display of souvenir fridge magnets) did not amount to his coincidence. It seemed the kind of flimsy coincidence that required a lot of drugs to prop it up. *Amplified*, he'd said earlier.

What drugs are you amplified on? I asked. (Now that we had settled, I wanted to be sure I would not be turning back, forfeiting the whole deal if in two hours he saw a dead opossum and took it as a bad omen.)

No drugs. Just off-brand quinapril, he said. For my heart.

And what's the matter with your heart?

Nothing, he said defensively. It just runs a little fast. I'm just fast-hearted, that's all.

Perhaps he had no health insurance, and was going to go fall down on the mercy of a Canadian hospital. I'd often thought of doing so myself, in the event that I ever broke a leg or anything serious. I imagined how I might fake painlessness at the border, disowning my agony, concealing any gory evidence for as long as it took to convince the guard. But of course that was out of the question, even hypothetically.

My heart, since you mention it, the once-drowned man

was saying now. Matter of fact, I haven't medicated it today. They tell you medication circulates better with a meal but everything I've eaten today has come from a vending machine. What about you—could you stomach something? We'll be needing gas, soon anyway, I see. Are you thirsty, at least? I don't want you running off the road with exhaustion. It's on me. The check and the time, they're both on me. He jogged whatever change was left in his suit pocket.

It was still dark, a little after 4 a.m. when we pulled into a roadhouse mated to a gas station.

The suitcase came inside with us. The little spruce stayed in the cab.

We sat on adjacent sides of one of the Formica tables. I sipped coffee and watched the once-drowned man order a burger. I watched him dismantle the burger with a knife and fork.

A knife and fork, I said.

I hate smelling onion on my hands, he explained. Also, it is prudent to disassemble preassembled foods, to ensure there are no malicious surprises. I tell you this from experience. Aren't you going to eat something? You left the meter on, didn't you?

Of course I had left the ticker on. I worshipped the ticker. (When we pulled in it had read $153 and change.) But I was trying, in these days I'm speaking of, not to worship the ticker quite so obviously. So I ordered buttered wheat toast and a side of scrambled eggs and a second cup of black coffee, while the once-drowned man told the story of how he had once drowned, in the Lower Niagara, on location for a movie that was never completed.

Probably for the best, he said, that this particular movie was never made. Wasn't very . . . au courant. Even for the times. Terrible casting, sketchy representations. Of which tribes, you might ask? I don't think even the screenwriter himself knew.

From the remaining scraps on his plate, the once-drowned man meticulously constructed a photogenic canapé. When he was done savoring this mouthful, he explained that one night he'd gone swimming after seven bad rounds of rummy and too many shots of rye, not reckoning on the current.

It was a Canadian fisherman hauled me out. Up early for the coho.

The once-drowned man laid down his knife and fork. He retrieved something crumpled from his pants pocket and smoothed it out on the table: a promotional flyer for a white-water rafting adventure. A man in a red sweatshirt stood on a rock in the middle of some rapids, directing just-in-frame rafts around his rock. All you had to do to be in the running was send in a bar code off a six-pack of Molson.

And this guy in the picture is your guy?

No. He sighed, folding the flyer away. It just got me to thinking of it. You must appreciate that serendipity is as much a state of awareness as it is one of synchronicity. I can give you the details, but they may not be deemed sufficient.

The competition was closed now, I noticed, and in any case he hadn't bought beer, only the seltzer.

And the spruce, I asked of the spruce.

It's a gift.

A gift.

I never did have a chance to thank him, the once-drowned man said. But I reckon I could find him pretty quick if I really tried. He could keep the tree small if he wanted to. Or if he has a yard he could plant it in the yard, a life that could grow up tall in front of him. Feels amiss, anyhow, not to thank.

Whether or not the man had a yard, it struck me as about the worst thing you could do to a person, reminding them that they were in some way responsible for you. I did not say this.

What other movies? I asked instead.

What do you mean, what other movies?

Movies you made.

I didn't make the movies, he said. I made the horses.

He obliged with a list of titles, but the names he gave meant nothing to me. In those days I often wished for a ready technology that allowed a person to instantly verify the grandiose claims of strangers, but that technology was still some years away. Our phones were just for phoning then, and it was safe to presume most people were full of smoke, but safer still not to call them on it.

He excused himself to make a phone call to the friend no longer in the habit of answering the phone. I went out to fuel the cab. While we'd been inside eating, the ticker had tripped past $163 and gave me a benevolent little wink as I climbed back in.

In a grass lot adjacent to the pumps, a circus was just

waking up. A huddle of domestic and exotic beasts, wreathed in the steam of their own breath. This was in the days when circuses still had animals, for better or (mostly) worse, and these ones looked ghostly in the still-dark morning, the pale stonewash of donkey coats soaking up the last of the moon.

My fare returned to the cab, suitcase in tow.

Did they pick up? I asked.

Would it hurt, he asked, just to sit a few minutes? Of course the meter . . .

I turned the ignition to get some heat back. The once-drowned man rubbed his hands vigorously with a wad of moist towelettes, peering out into the dark, where a one-hump camel stood grooming her knobbly calf.

I had been to a circus only once, when I was about eleven. Probably they had animals at that one too, but I don't remember any. The only act I remember clearly is a woman being hooked by her shining black hair to a trapeze wire, then being lifted and swung around the tent. Right before her toes left the ground the tension elongated her eyes shockingly. Then she was up. She looked much younger in flight, her face pulled taut by the wire.

Supreme face-lift, my mother leaned in to whisper. She sat beside me, at the back of the grandstand, rolling an unlit Alpine cigarette between her long fingers. She had only just come back to us, from wherever it was she had been, and was wearing a coat made of gray and white rabbits. Or possibly gray-and-white rabbits. This coat had deep, deep pockets I liked to sneak my hands into, even though all I ever found were disintegrating tissues and stray breath mints and ticket stubs from cinemas and dog tracks. It didn't matter—I wasn't fishing for any prizes. I liked to just slide my hand in and leave it there. I wanted to be sure she wouldn't vanish again, float right off, and she never liked to hold directly to my sticky paws.

The circus woman's legs cycled the air as she rose, as though pedaling an invisible bike, up and up. The wire hooked into her hair was operated by a couple of men, tucked away in the shadows of the big top. White open-necked peasant shirts, sleeves rolled up thick forearms. They were responsible for hoisting her up, hand over hand, swift and smooth. Nearer the top some mechanism released, and she began to twirl, was twirled in place, like a figure skater, fast enough to blur, her smile fixed rigid and her teeth bared. I wondered: if she were to let her expression falter the slightest bit, might her scalp just tear right off?

How can she smile like that? I asked my mother. It must hurt so bad.

It must hurt so bad, my mother repeated. Jesus. You want to know how a woman might still be able to smile while she's being swung around by her hair? That's a useful thing to know, kitten. How about we go ask her after they let her down? If you're all right with learning something a little earlier than you're meant to.

She had left us because my father suffered from something

she called "terminal cowardice," complicated by chronic neediness, and I wanted to show that none of this cowardice or neediness had found its way into my blood. Of course it had.

*

The ticker ticked over to $171. A boy in gold lamé tights came out of his caravan to brush down a pair of horses.

Son pequeños caballos, said the once-drowned man. Got a bit of Mongolian in them, looks like. Bigger than Mongol ponies though. Mutts. I've always preferred working with mutts. People and animals both. Can be as stubborn and haughty as blue bloods, but they possess better instincts. I've thought about it, and I'd say it comes from living between identities. From always having to measure, here to there, this to that. What about you, Blessed Katherine-with-a-K, does that hold water? Here, lemme ask them.

He wound down the window and poked his head into the cold blue air. He made a blustery horse noise—a nickering, very convincing—and the horses raised their handsome heads. One took a couple of steps towards us and the boy in lamé stilled it with a sweet sleepy word.

Well. The once-drowned man wound the window back up, eyes brightened. Still got something.

The air became denser the farther north we got. I watched it growing viscous in the high beams. The smell of pine resin came in through the ventilation, and the little spruce quivered as if in response.

The early light seemed fruit-colored and well-meaning. We went by pasture in which there were no animals, only out-of-commission billboards. I could just make out the words on one of them, a passage quoted from Kings, about the remnant of the Sodomites being expelled from the land. The lettering had faded to sugary pastels, as of an invitation to an Easter picnic, or an advertisement for baby clothes. It brought the taste of stale marzipan.

The once-drowned man read aloud from the board.

God, they make it hard, do they not, Katherine?

Then the once-drowned man told me of how he had once drowned, in the Lower Niagara, a nineteen-year-old stunt rider from the Okanagan.

Maybe I would have pulled over, if there had been any place to pull over. There was no place. Instead I drove in silence with great shelves of understanding shearing away, as he rushed on to reassure me that it had not been his intent to drown the rider.

I had thought that I could swim, he pleaded, please know that. I had thought the kid could swim, growing up rural and all. But then the riverbed dropped away. And the current, as I have already mentioned. And it was late, very dark, after a long day on set, and we had both had some too many.

Canned, of course, he went on, in answer to my silence. That film was canned.

I let a mile or two slip past before I spoke up.

You told me it was yourself, I said. Yourself who drowned.

He seemed relieved, even grateful, to elaborate, straighten the record. Yes, me as well, he said. I clutched, if you will, the proverbial straw. And the stunt rider, the Okanagan, was in fact a little wick of a thing, though still, you'd have thought that swimming was crucial in the profession. We were down, we were both down, then I was on my own. Thrashing, who knows how long. Then someone fished me out. This Canadian fisherman, ex–mounted police, as I have mentioned. Jawline like so. (He drew a 110-degree angle in the air between us.) That's all I remember.

It was my fear he was talking to, I understood. He spoke as if to chase fear from the cab, to exhaust it like a harmful gas. But he would not allow me a clear image of the rider.

Was there something between you? I tried, to no definite response. Then: Did you have some kind of falling-out?

Eventually he replied.

The manner between the rider and myself was nothing but companionable. However. There was the complicated misinterpretation of my wristwatch and favorite boots, my paycheck being discovered within the Okanagan's trailer. Losing these things had seemed trivial at the time of losing them. Good riddance, boots, I thought. Good riddance, TAG Heuer. But my nonattachment in that regard was ultimately not to my advantage. In the minds of others, the loss of these things amounted to motive.

In the passenger seat the once-drowned man held his own slender wrist, as a brace or a manacle, or in memory of his TAG Heuer. Possibly as a measure of pulse. His heart, I wondered.

But I know this story, I told him. Something like it happened in a movie.

Did it? He looked pained. I never heard about that one.

It was recent, I said. A couple of years ago.

There you go, he said. Vampires, everywhere. But it's still my story.

He continued telling it, a little speedier now, yanking his life back from the clutches of Hollywood bloodsuckers.

They say that I was in a true fugue state for a while, when they finally pumped the river out of me. Babbling around and around with remorse. Remorse: that was noted, remorse was on the record, all the way through. Whatever else might have remained in question. I was even happy to do the time. Or I thought it about right. Unavoidable. Only.

Here he petted the little spruce.

Only, I just didn't think I'd do so much of it. I wrote the kid's folks once or twice, from inside. To say how sorry. To explain. They wrote me back a few times. Sometimes they said they understood it was an accident, and that they hoped the Lord might grant me peace. Other times they said that they knew it was an accident, but even so they sometimes wished I'd been given the chair, or been injected with a terminal virus or slow-acting poison. I don't think this was intended as malicious, to hurt the way it did. I think somebody professional had instructed them to say whatever was in their hearts.

Well, he said. It wasn't a complete wash. I learned how to play scopa and ombre, and picked up a little Slovene from a very genial defrauder. I read half of Proust, and all of Baldwin, and the poems of Anna Akhmatova, only in a language she did not intend for them to rhyme in. Think I got the gist, though. He brought his fingers to his face to smell the pine sap.

My eyes ached with middle distance. Every time I relaxed them, a deer or a family of deer would appear at the verge, ready to spring. I remember the deer seemed especially orange that year. It might have been the vegetation, whatever they were eating, or else something in the water. It might have been some particulate matter in the atmosphere that accentuated their orangeness. It might of course have only been my mind, my eyes.

The once-drowned man went quiet awhile, after that. Spent of something. In periphery he seemed diminished, shrunk down inside his shabby jacket. When I turned and looked, I saw his eyes had closed, and his mouth hung slack. His heart, I wondered again, but his breathing sounded regular. I drove and he stayed that way. I switched on the radio; I swerved heroically to avoid a silver baroque sofa, filthy but miraculous, which must have fallen from a truck or been dragged out from the woods into the middle of the interstate.

His head knocked sickly against the window glass, but he never stirred. I suspected he might be pretending, as a test of my good faith. I let him sleep or pretend to sleep, well past his collateral. All the way up to four hundred, where whatever there was of my good faith ran out. I took the exit for a grim skyline, and coasted the town until I found a bank. There was the first snow I saw that year, already dead and plowed into greasy heaps in the gutters. I pulled into the bank's empty lot, unsure whether the institution mattered. Trading hours hadn't started yet, but there was movement behind the dark windows.

I cut the ignition and the radio died. He woke with a start, like a child after a long drive home from Grandma's.

And where are we?

I told him.

And what're we at? He waved at the ticker. My eyes haven't started.

I told him. I was including the way back, and the tip.

Allora, he said glumly.

Inside the bank someone flipped the OPEN sign.

Let's see how this plays, he said, and got out with a sheaf of papers. I could see him thinking about taking the suitcase, saw him see me see him thinking it. Instead he repositioned it on the passenger seat, gave it another busted look, and closed the door very gently.

He shuffled across the parking lot towards the bank, his suit looking exactly like he'd slept in it, and went inside. From where I was sitting I could only see the cab reflected in the dark tint of the windows, and me or the shade of me behind another layer of tint, so I can't tell you what I looked like in this moment. I sat out there waiting. Longer than I should have, it's true. Telling myself, I won't belittle myself by going in, I won't belittle myself by going in, as other cars crept through the slush into the lot.

*

My mother had given me a little shove in the direction of that trapeze woman, after the show, telling me she'd wait. But I was either too shy or too wary of leaving her side.

She'd raked her hand through her hair, curls held stiff with sugar water.

Well, maybe you're too young anyway. Twelve? I don't know, when I was twelve I was riding alone out to . . . well. She went quiet and looked at me. It doesn't matter, she said. I'm sorry. I'm just not very good at this shit.

Not long after that she was gone again. My father and I spent a couple more years looking over the table at each other. Sometimes our eyes met and I imagined the conversation our eyes were having, things we would never say out loud:

She loved me first, you know.

Yes, but she loved me best.

To be honest I don't think either of us would have hesitated to throw the other under the bus, if it meant pleasing her for half a minute. But we were what we had, he and I, and all told we were both gentle, careful people who could not help being mostly gentle and careful with each other.

Still, I moved away at fifteen, as far as I could get.

*

The bank's parking lot filled steadily with cars. I reached over to the suitcase and flipped its yellowed luggage tag. The address side was blank and the airline had, if I recalled correctly, been bankrupted years before. I got out of the cab to stretch my legs. I stretched my legs past the windows of the bank several times before I finally saw him through the dark glass, waving his hands and his documents in front of a clerk. I went back to the cab.

I knew he was not coming out of there with any money. Even so, it felt shabby, looking through that suitcase. I found nothing of any value in it. Another change of clothes, and several years of a subscription to a movie magazine. Something soft wrapped in yellow tissue, that I thought better of opening. A Greyhound bus ticket from the day before, that had brought him all the way upstate, presumably to meet the friend who had not shown. Addresses for houses of charity several hundred miles behind us.

I zipped it all back and stood the case in the next empty parking space, where he could easily notice it once he came back out. It looked very vulnerable standing there alone. Vulnerable and suspicious at the same time. I worried over someone else getting to it first. Overall I felt better when it was settled back in the passenger side.

In the rearview mirror I watched him picking his way back between cars.

I'm sorry, he said, approaching my window. My accounts, they're still thawing. I'll understand if you . . . He lifted his chin, showing sincere razor burn. If the sky holds I could maybe even walk the rest of the way.

Just get in, I said.

I can send you the rest, he offered. When my checkbooks are ready. You can write down your address . . .

I told him we could sort it out later, though later I would neglect to do this. I don't remember if I was spooked by the possibility of him calling by in person—turning up on the doorstep with a cage of canaries or a salt lamp or who knows what—or whether I already knew that the address would be short-lived, that by the time he sent the money, I wouldn't be the one opening the envelope.

Just get in, I said again, with a disgust I did not really feel, having half-expected all along, I realized now, to be wrung in one way or another.

He got in and closed the door very quietly, as though trying not to wake something. Again he made himself small in the passenger seat, shrugged deep into his jacket, as if taking up less space might compensate for the shortfall. But he proved unwilling or unable to abide by the common laws of contrition.

You've seen the Falls before, he said. We had barely reentered the interstate.

Once, I told him, nudging the cab into the traffic.

Good. So you know it's fake.

Fake. Fake as in how?

Fake as in it doesn't naturally look how it looks. They got these big stone pillars upriver, and they raise them up and down to orchestrate the waterflow, so that it falls in a nicer curtain. (He made a smooth show with his hands.) Looks prettier, more dramatic for the spectators. Nature shouldn't be like that, nature shouldn't have spectators. It isn't the sports.

Who controls these pillars? I could not help myself from asking. The Canadians or the Americans?

The Americans, of course. Doesn't it sound like American meddling to you? The Canadians are satisfied with nature being nature. But it's supposed to look better from the Canadian side in the first place, so maybe the Americans are just leveling the playing field.

We were passing an amusement park. I glimpsed the snaking coaster-track in the rearview, rising above the cyclone and razor wire, internment camp fencing. It was a disgraced amusement park. A couple of years beforehand a kid had died when his seat dropped from the Ferris wheel.

What if you were to curl up in back, he proposed, and I were to drive us across?

And even if that works, I said. How would I get back?

Back, he repeated, as if it were an unsavory word. But why would any of us want to get back?

Much later I would look up the movie titles he had mentioned, as I remembered them, to find that they were real but not well known, and none had survived the leap to digital.

On the road ahead of us, vehicles began dancing between lanes in anxious choreography. I pulled off before we got within sight of the border boxes, behind a silver station wagon. The wagon was packed to the roof rack, five seats to the family of seven. North Carolina plates. The mother and oldest girl were fishing their passports and jackets out from the chaos, preparing to walk across on foot.

Looks like my party, the once-drowned man said. He

opened the passenger door and set his suitcase on the blacktop. Reaching in for the spruce tree, he hesitated.

I expect they won't let it across, will they?

I told him that probably it came from Canada in the first place. From those French Canadian woodsmen who drive down to Manhattan in their Christmas tree vans and get laid like carpet.

But maybe you should keep it, he said. As a token.

I don't have a garden where I live.

These never tend to grow very tall, he promised. These potted ones. Like goldfish you win at the fair. For some reason they always seem to stay runted. Will probably only reach to about five and a half feet.

Tall enough, I said. I'm five and a half feet.

There you go, he said. Kismet.

He thanked and thanked and thanked, then trundled the suitcase in the wake of the mother and daughter, towards the line of guard boxes. At one point he looked back and gave a little flop of a wave. It seemed bad luck to watch him cross. Or I told myself it would be bad luck to watch him cross. In truth I suspect I only wanted to escape responsibility for him if they bounced him back.

It would be fair and easy to say that I was made anxious by the possibility of questions, by the real possibility of requests for various corresponding documents I would not be able to produce, of untold hours in uncomfortable plastic chairs alongside nervous families trying to keep their tired bored children from expressing their tired boredom.

And I was. Made anxious of these things.

But there was something else running underneath. A queasy complicity in whatever he'd done or was yet to do.

I sped back across Grand Island, past the disgraced amusement park, window down to let the cold keep me awake and to scour away some of my sense of wrongdoing. Down on the floor of the passenger side, the little spruce tree hushed softly again in the draft. *Susurrus, susurrus*, it would say if it did happen to grow tall, but for now it could only manage *sus*.

By the time I passed the circus lot, the sun was high, or high for December, there throbbing at my temple like a thought demanding entry.

I pulled up to where the horses stood shimmying a little way from the fence, flanks brilliant in the winter glare, the very dust in their coats winking like mica.

Pequeños caballos, I tried, then made a kissing noise from the window. The horses tilted their rowboat ears but wouldn't come.

The smell of chaff baking in sunlight remained faithful to my mother, would always be faithful to my mother: surely too hot in her rabbit coat, luminous green eyes burning like a chemical fire fed by smeary wicks of kohl. The trapeze woman's smile had grown savage as she'd twirled—was twirled—faster and faster, unfurling her billowing sleeves and letting sequins rain down like sparks. The sequins had seemed to spill straight from her veins, biblical, falling right into our hands, into our own untortured hair, glinting onto the parched pine boards beneath our feet. There must have been no net. For the sake of seventy-five people in a small village I promise you'll never hear about, there was no net, and the trapeze woman had smiled in spite of us, or because of us, or to damn us all to eternity exactly where we stood.

There might've been a thousand things my mother had wished for me to learn, waiting outside with her gold stilettos planted in the straw. But probably there was just the one. I still hoped I might recover it.

A Small Cleared Space

She'd set out later than she'd planned to, the four o'clock sun already sinking at her shoulder, threatening to drop behind the mountains and plunge the world into gloaming. For now the surrounding woods were lit gold, and frost bloomed inside her visor. Snow was banked up on both sides of the trail like a luge run, and she raced the ATV over other people's tracks, trying to beat the coming dark. On either side the pines stood solemn, branches clotted, cradling snow.

The hourglass pond was nicotine at its edges, ice all the way to the opposite bank. Strange for this time of year, but the freeze had come early, following a string of freak lows and silver thaws, and Uncle Wish had assured her it was solid at the narrows and fine for driving on.

On the far bank his and Iona's cabin crouched cowed in a small cleared space. It wasn't an especially pretty thing to look at, just a boxy one-room with a single-pitch roof, built of whatever Wish and her father could salvage and haul out here in the seventies. Its beauty was in its remoteness, its inaccessibility. There were two months of the year when it was entirely cut off, when the ice was either breaking up or still too thin to risk putting a foot on, let alone a bike. Even in the warmer months, the cabin had a solitude that had to be earned; a boat would have to be towed in behind an ATV along the ten kilometers of half-strangled trail.

One summer she'd brought Emile home to meet everyone, and the two of them had swum across to the cabin on a whim, each paddling one-handed, holding the neck of a liquor bottle, with Emile towing a makeshift foamboard raft piled up with their clothes and cigarettes.

Naoishe had turned on her back and swum otter-like to watch him coming, the raft's rope between his teeth like a limp weasel. *Big smiley bird dog*, she remembers thinking.

She'd called out, Why do you have to do everything the hard way? and he'd tried to respond but the rope made it impossible. Now she wondered what the words might have been.

Naoishe set her teeth together and coaxed the ATV onto the ice. There was a slight groan beneath the tires, something she could feel rather than hear; a viscous fear in the belly, like when the floor drops out from a carnival ride. She held her breath and thumbed the throttle. In a month's time the entire pond system would be lidded over with three feet of ice, and people would ride their snowmobiles all the way to St. John's.

A few years earlier a kid ran out of fuel trying to get to his father's house in Witless Bay. He was found eight kilometers from the broken-down machine, curled up like he was sleeping. Last Christmas someone brought it up, how they'd seen his mother at the Costco, eyes like collapsed burrows, buying milk and macaroni dinner as if life were still worth living. Shame on her.

Oh, come on—you can't know. Emile had defended the woman. Who's gonna keep their kids under surveillance twenty-four seven?

The aunts had flashed the look, the "outsider" look, to which Emile was thankfully either oblivious or indifferent. Later Naoishe had drawn her arms across her body, spoken aloud to her daughter through the muffle of wool and blood: Listen, you in there. Once you get out here I am never going to let you go.

Did Emile blame her, her body? No, of course not. Of course not. He'd held her tight by the shoulders and spoken close to her face. It was not her fault. She'd done everything right. They'd be more careful next time.

More careful, she thought. *Less careless*. It sounded, to her, like blame.

At Thanksgiving he'd flown back alone to his family in Saguenay, and she'd encouraged him to stay on there. That was mid-October. Then the leftover jack-o'-lanterns were deflating, up and down neighboring porches, and raccoons had moved back into the roof in preparation for the cold. Among Emile's texts were reminders for her to take the car in for snow tires.

Naoishe had carried a box of his winter clothes to the post office and had it shipped express.

This is crazy, he called to say. But he'd stayed up there to meet the package, and the ones that followed.

A footnote to a bad year, to this other disaster. She realized she felt just as cut off either way: alone in their Toronto apartment, curled up on the couch, chipping away at an Everest of backlogged emails (condolences, check-ins, appeals to go back to teaching other people's children how to read, how to write, how to twist pipe cleaners into vague animal shapes); or the same thing, but with Emile pottering around in the background, trying to get her to eat things, drink things, laugh at things. These were two kinds of the same aloneness.

And this third kind, this middle-of-a-frozen-lake aloneness? It wasn't so different. But there was something satisfying, even comforting in the magnitude of surrounds, the physical apartness. It seemed important to feel small.

The quad carried her over the bank, up onto land, and she parked it in the open-faced shed that housed firewood and a diesel generator. Naoishe shook her hands out of her riding mitts and felt behind a fuel can for the key, hoisted the panniers off the bike and dragged them across the snowy clearing to the cabin's door. She fumbled the key against the lock, her hands stupid with the cold.

She'd been expecting a friendly, musty squalor, the familiar disorder from her teenage visits, but she shoved the door open on a room that was prepped as if for a paying guest. Iona must've sent Uncle Wish out there that same day, or perhaps—it was possible, given the situation—he had thought to go himself. One of the bunk beds that lined the back wall was already made up with pillows and three layers of blankets. A few logs were stacked beside the woodstove and a nest of kindling waited to be lit. On the table a yellow checkered tea towel swaddled a fresh loaf of dense molasses rye, and next to it a note read, *Dear Neesh, Welcome!* followed by bullet-point instructions for the new generator.

From the panniers Naoishe unpacked the supplies she'd brought out, adding them to the pantry. The shelves were already stacked with field rations, as her uncle called them—tins of things that could be eaten cold if worse came to worst and there was no fuel, neither dry wood nor propane. Canned tuna, beans, pasta dinners. Bomb shelter food. There were also the perennial jars of home-preserved meat, replenished each fall when somebody got his moose. Metal screw-top lids corroding with spilled brine. Through the glass, Naoishe saw the stringy pink meat and die-sized lumps of white fat. Strange webbing, like something preserved a long time ago in formaldehyde. She hid them behind tins of chili and Italian wedding soup, foods whose contents were embellished by bright paper labels.

While there were a few shreds of light left she went out to meet the generator, and startled a cat hunkered down amidst the pile of birch logs. A cub-sized black thing, yellow-eyed, its flattened ears finishing in owlish tufts. She hadn't noticed it when she parked the bike, but it must have been there. Now it crouched yowling over a stumbling brood of half-blind kittens.

Stupid time of the year to be having babies, she told it. Don't they teach you that in wildcat school? But the cat only spat more viciously, and the kittens, if they survived through to March, would grow into vicious things too. Wish would've shot the cat and melted a bucket of snow just to drown the kittens. *Fer der own good.*

Fine, she said, coaxing the generator into life before carefully extracting an armload of firewood from the cat's adopted fort. *Bonne nuit.*

The body has no memory for pain. She'd read that somewhere and believed it true. Now she knew it to be. The year had been an agonizing parade of firsts, and at each her grief had astonished her. She wondered if it would be easier to have something definitive to point to, an instance of physical impact; slipping in a wet stairwell, falling from a bike, getting rear-ended at an intersection. But then there would just be different whys, equally useless, and there would still have been enough room for guilt, cunning shape-shifter that it is, to creep in at the edges.

When she'd come home from the hospital she found that Emile had pushed all of the baby's things into the spare room—that's what it was demoted to, *spare*—and locked the door.

Have you set up a hydroponics lab in there? she asked. She felt equal measures of pity and disgust at him thinking he could screen her from any of it. It was his loss too, she knew, but not his failure. It was not his body that seemed simultaneously to mourn and to deny the loss of the child, producing milk, making provisions where none were needed.

Come on, she said, I'm not a fucking kid. He gave her a wounded look along with the keys, and she went in there and wailed amidst the crib, the bassinet, the pastel drifts of bunny rugs and soft animals. Couldn't it at least have happened sooner? Before they were fitted out with all this *stuff*? Of course the stores took things back under such circumstances, some sort of policy, but who had the energy? Other people, apparently. Her brother-in-law Jacob had come with the truck, while her sister Molly had helped sort through the receipts and credit card statements. The gifts though, the hand-knitted giraffes and mittens and red felt Mary Janes—what could you do with those? Hold on to them, Molly said. You'll try again. It's hard to think about now, but you will. And Naoishe had nodded, knowing she wouldn't.

From one of the water bottles she filled a saucepan and set it on the stove, stirring in a few tablespoons of powdered milk as it heated. When the milk had dissolved she splashed a little into a saucer and left it outside the door for the cat to find. To the rest she added cocoa and peppermint sugar, then rolled a thin joint from the pot Jacob had snuck her at Christmas, when she'd told him she wasn't sleeping so well.

Hot chocolate and cheeba; a passport to seventeen. She wanted the soundtrack that went along with it, *Blacklisted* or *The Greatest* on the stereo, something she knew all the words and could sing to, lose her shit just a little bit.

But there was no sound system out here save an old radio and a portable cassette player with a modest assemblage of tapes and dead batteries. She fell asleep to the CBC, waking at midnight to the dampened thuds of fireworks going off in the village, and remembering: New Year's Eve. Like a child she went over to the window. Across the pond the trees looked soft, naked maple and dogberry with branches furred at the edges, like velvet antler fuzz. She waited and heard another smatter of distant explosions, but none of the shed-made roman candles or the store-bought jitterbugs made it above the sooty tree line. There was just the faint glow of them spread through the dense sky, and she took herself back to bed.

In the morning she opened the door and saw the milk was still there, now solid and opaque in its saucer. The cat didn't trust her, and why should it? It had gotten this far. Still, she felt rebuffed.

The day was bright and clear. *A good day for it*, came a man's voice in the back of her mind, falsely cheerful. She thought she recognized the voice as her father's or grandfather's, she wasn't sure. She pressed—*a good day for what, exactly?*—but no response came.

New Year's Day, the last of the firsts. A year ago she'd woken to the smell of frying potatoes and eggs, Emile cooking a hangover breakfast despite the mutual lack of hangover—Look, he said, there's a right way and a wrong way to start a year. The right way is smash browns. He'd pointed a spatula at her. Back to bed, I'll bring a tray. But this morning she cut a doorstop slice from the molasses rye and folded it over itself to eat while getting dressed.

Which film had been playing at the Royal that evening? It seemed impossible that she could not remember this now, when she remembered so many other details: the pale gray winter dress (now ruined, thrown out), the face of the usherette, the smell of popcorn left to burn.

Miss? You're, uhm . . .

Emile's hands shaking as he tried to turn his cell back on. Somewhere, perhaps, in a coat pocket or a wallet, there were ticket stubs.

Stepping down from the cabin and into the snow she listened to the pines overhead, brittle with frozen sap and creaking like the rigging on a ship. She'd come out with vague ideas of ceremony, memorial. A package of tiny woolens, knitted animals, an engraved silver spoon. She wasn't sure what she would do. What was fitting. Something would present itself. Years ago she'd read about cultures who buried babies in the hollows of trees, then sealed them over with mud or resin. Something like that. Or else she was going to take the hand auger out to the middle of the pond and drill a hole there, feed each item through to the water beneath, the tiny clothes in peach and pink, the toy giraffe, the silver spoon.

But it all seemed pointless now. Stupid. Leaving things to rot and tarnish in a squirrel hole or in the lonely dark of the pond. She knew there'd be no comfort in it.

Eight months. That close. She felt like howling. She might howl. This was a place where she could howl. Instead she said her name and it sounded just as forlorn. Her own name, as though calling herself back from the treacherous edge of something. It was involuntary, this utterance, this name-noise, and so she guessed this must be the purpose of it: *come back, come back, get away from there.*

She brushed snow off the step and sat, feeling the bulk of the package under her coat. The weight of a child asleep on her chest—it was something she'd been looking forward to. The nurses had put the baby there for a minute, and in the year since she'd often found herself reaching up and pressing her hand against the spot, trying to reproduce the exact pressure.

Across the clearing the cat emerged from the woodpile, carrying a kitten in its mouth. It ran across the snow on stocky legs, giving Naoishe and the cabin a wide berth, its bedraggled little bundle swinging pendulously.

Naoishe watched as it trotted out across the ice, wondering what safer place it could have found.

Horse Latitudes

Somebody has that job, but we never catch sight of him. In the morning we'll roll out to bloody drag marks at the side of the highway. Doesn't matter how early I get up, dismantle the tent. Knock on the door of the Cardinal to rattle Thea awake before going in to put coffee on the stove.

You decent? I'll call out.

Sure, I'm decent, she'll call back, in her best Rita Hayworth. I'll climb in and she'll be sitting up, almost queenly in the unmade bed. Her voice will still be husky with sleep, and while I wrestle the ancient gas range into life, she'll slip my boots on over her pajama pants and trudge out to the brick shower block. Lope back zipped into skinny jeans with a silk scarf tied over her damp hair just as I'm pouring the coffee into travel mugs.

I'll ease the truck onto the recurring dream of the Eyre Highway as early as seven, sometimes before, but he'll have already been through—some poor bastard hefting shovelfuls of last night's marsupial gore into the tray of a tonner, and continuing on across the Nullarbor. Going home to his wife and kids smelling of dead things.

This morning a pair of eagles are picking what's left off the road, stretching sinewy strips of flesh between claw and beak.

Jesus, behold the bloody majesty, Thea says from behind her sunglasses, turning her head from the passenger window. Didn't know they were scavengers.

She has the map across her knees. It's been unfolded and refolded so many times that Lake Gilmore is just a hole where four creases used to meet.

Go straight, she tells me. Go east. She's said this every hundred kilometers since Norseman, and probably won't stop saying it till we reach Ceduna. All her jokes are dad jokes, old-man jokes (*Pleased to meet you, Hungry, I'm Thirsty. You feel like a pie? You don't look like a pie.*). I go ahead and laugh for her anyway.

At Balladonia I feed fuel to the truck while Thea wanders through the roadhouse's exhibition of Skylab wreckage, gleaned from the few dozen tons of dead space station sprinkled over the Nullarbor in the seventies. She leans in close to glass cabinets filled with pieces that fell to earth intact—a freezer, a hatch door, an oxygen tank—and other detritus that the atmosphere twisted and scorched beyond recognition.

She looks as out of place here as the space junk. Her blunt black bob, the painted-on jeans showing how little there is left of her. Big-city skinny, heartbreak skinny; I can't tell which. The Cartier that Thiago gave her is still strapped to her wrist, but her wedding and engagement rings she pitched into the river at Crawley the night before we left Perth.

He always hated this city, she'd said, as the ripples traveled out to the bank to meet us. He'd hate to think his diamonds are in the mud at the bottom of the Swan.

Here it is: I threw rice at their wedding. Tied streamers and beer cans to the back of their beautiful rented Daimler and waved them off, gardenias wilting in her hair, sweat patches under the arms of his handmade Kilgour suit. The whole time I had this picture in my head. Tabloid headlines from the front-page newspaper grates in the window of a newsagency twenty years before. Words like WEDDING TRAGEDY and NEWLYWEDS' DISASTER in eight-inch lettering, and the mangled wreck of a white sedan, a tin piñata broken open, scattering wedding gifts across a slick black highway. Glassware and linen and electric knives and fondue sets. Creamy tulle frothing from the passenger side, or did I imagine that part? Even in my head, the image is brittle, overhandled, because I couldn't leave it alone, couldn't stop worrying at it. Because nobody holds on to something for nothing, right?

In the end, Thea and Thiago's disaster was so mediocre that even *The West* wouldn't have run it. They didn't last two years together, didn't even make it to cotton.

Thea doesn't share the gritty details of how things shook apart. There was the apartment in Buenos Aires, seven rooms all with yellow curtains and too many amaryllis plants, their flowers like cartoon megaphones. *Can't seem to keep these damned things alive.* She wrote that on a postcard last September, one that showed the Recoleta Cemetery and said, *PS—wish you were here.* That's all I know about her life there. She speaks in half-sentences, trying to explain what it was like to come back to Perth on her own. Pulling up the roller door on the storage unit, on all the furniture she thought she'd one day send for, the boxes she'd padded out with blankets, worried they'd be thrown around the shipping container during its trip across the Pacific.

I really thought that . . . I mean it wasn't just . . . You know I went in and I opened these drawers expecting to find. I don't know. Some kind of. I don't know. Some kind of advice from the person who packed it all up.

You mean you? I ask.

Yeah, me, she says. Felt like my life had pretty much shrunk to fit that space. Like I could go in and pull the door down behind me and no one would ever come looking.

Instead of entombing herself for all eternity in an eight-by-ten at King's Storage, she'd bought the Cardinal from a widower in Mount Hawthorn. It was a cigar-smelling relic upholstered in brown and orange floral, lined with forty-year-old copies of *Parade*. She'd aired the thing out for a couple of weeks, replaced the musty foam mattress and the gas bottle, but left the soft sixties pornography soaking the damp from the cupboards. Then she'd called me.

Chef, she said. What's cooking?

Took your time, I said. Nice of you to check in and all.

Forgive me, she said, not a question. Heard you're driving to Melbourne next week.

And from whom did you hear that?

Your truck, she pressed, undeterred. It has a tow bar, yes?

So that's it. Hitching yourself to the nearest available wagon. As per.

A pause on her end of the line. Too soon, I realized, and to smooth things down I asked what the tare weight was.

Tare weight, she repeated.

How heavy.

Not so heavy, it's just one of those—what do they call it—a canned ham?

Canned ham. All right, Ham. But we're pushing straight through, no sightseeing, minimal piss stops. I'm offshore end of month.

Maersk still owns your bones, then, she said.

Only till the oil dries up. Don't you be getting lofty on me, deserter.

And I suppose I shouldn't ask why you're going to drive four thousand klicks, then turn around and drive right back again. Working holiday?

Well, as of now, if anyone asks, I'm helping out a mate.

Which mate is that?

As of right now that's you, Skittles for breakfast.

When we get to Victoria she'll put the Cardinal up on blocks on her sister's farm, somewhere out in the alluvial fields. Spend time feeding horses and walking the dry creek while she waits for her life to come find her. Me, if I'm lucky there'll be a couple of days left for me to lie on my brother's couch with his kid and cats on my chest. Real-life tourism. That's if we ever make it that far. I feel the Cardinal lagging behind the Ranger, dragging air, its resistance to momentum. I feel if I put my foot down too quick I'll rip the chassis right out from under it, leave another ruin for the landscape to claim as its own. Wrecks are strewn through the scrub like strange sculptures, some of them torched, some of them sifting quietly back to the earth, flake by rusty flake. Every now and then there'll be a fresh one; license plates gone but the duco still bright under the layer of Nullarbor dust.

Thirty kilometers out of Caiguna, Thea asks me to pull over. So I pull over, thinking she needs to either throw up or find a convenient patch of scrub. She jumps down from the passenger side and takes the tire iron from the back. In the rearview I watch her run back to a red Nissan, forty meters off the highway. No plates. ID number scratched off if they knew what they were doing. Thea circles the car, scoping it out as though she's going to raid the loose change from its ashtray. She puts her face against the driver-side window, then walks around to the back and jams the iron under the lid of the boot, prying it open with a few swift pumps of her slender arms. The boot gapes, and I see the slouch in Thea's shoulders, but can't tell what it means. Disappointment? Relief? She leaves the car yawning in the hot wind and lopes back to the Ranger, tugging the scarf from her hair to dab sweat from her face and neck. I hear the tire iron clank into the bed before she slumps into the passenger seat.

What'd you find?

Nothing, she says, wiping grease on her jeans.

What were you hoping you'd find?

Nothing, she says again. I was hoping I'd find nothing. Let's just drive, hey?

She paws through the glove box for a CD, settles on something mournful and wordless, and I think that will be the end of it. But we stop again for a deserted Excel just past Madura, and twice more between there and Mundrabilla. Each time it's the same thing; watching Thea's back as she jogs towards the Honda Civic, then the old Datsun Bluebird, swinging the tire iron at her side like some post-apocalyptic vigilante. But she has some trouble with the Datsun, can't jemmy the boot. I watch her growing larger in the rearview as she comes back and leans in the passenger window, resting her head on her sweaty forearms.

Can you give me a hand?

What is it? I ask her. What exactly are you doing?

Like you said. It just makes me. Uneasy.

Her own eight-inch headlines. Her own mental scrapbook of gruesome tabloid clutter. All the terrible things the mind spits up when it's given enough space.

No more, I tell her. Come on, get in.

She lifts her head, but that's all.

Look, I say, I don't think you understand. The chopper leaves on the twenty-third, with or without me. And if I miss this hitch, I'm twelve grand down. I don't know if that means anything to someone who throws diamonds into a river, but it means something to me.

Okay, she says. No more, I get it. But it's as though the words have snapped free of their meaning. I understand, she says. No more after this one. But can you just give me another two minutes?

Thea uses her two minutes to do impressive violence to the Datsun, taking out all six windows, the headlights and taillights, sending the wing mirrors skittering into the scrub before turning on the shell and leaving fist-sized dents in the metal. I watch the arc and sweep of the tire iron and I remember how she used to dance. Her efforts ring out across the still air, the empty sky, and her rage seems piteously small against that hugeness.

All this trip I've been watching her, thinking that it might be that simple; stepping out of your life as if stepping out of a lift and onto an unfamiliar floor, adjusting your gait to something purposeful. As if it could be like that, clean and easy, just the hum of the unseen cables lingering in your ears, a little vertigo and the floors below forgotten, flooded for all you know or care.

But it isn't clean or easy. I'm figuring out how I'm going to get in between her and the car she's attacking without losing any jawbone, when she finally lowers the iron. She takes one more swing at a fender for good measure, then looks at her Cartier. Looks back at me. Holds up two fingers.

I say nothing as she climbs back into the passenger side, her face all salt and dust and snot, her silk top sticking to her skin. She closes her eyes and after a few minutes her breathing shallows and slows. When we were kids she'd sleep in my bed, too wasted on Toohey's Old and Hyde Park punk to make it back to her own. I'd find her whichever T-shirt was smallest and cleanest—an ironic op-shop find, *Dog Swamp Bowls Club*—and she'd stand there and change right in front of me. There was the tattoo of the red bird perched on her hipbone, kept secret from her parents. There were her martini-glass tits. *Any more than a handful's a waste, right?* Did she know what she was doing? In bed she'd fling her limbs out in the dark, get an arm and a leg over me like I was something she wanted to climb. Sleep-talking drunk with her wet mouth against my shoulder, *C'mere you.*

But nothing ever came of it. She met Thiago in her second year of uni. He was older than us, in Western Australia for god knows why—did they not have biological arts, or whatever he was mastering, in the other hemisphere? Then it was ten years of pretending I liked the guy. No, I did like him, or I would have, if things had been different. But he had a lot of money and he had Thea. I maybe could've stood one or the other, but both was too much, the salt and the wound.

Twenty minutes from the border I pull into the Eucla roadhouse and leave Thea sleeping while I search the truck and the caravan for rogue fruit. I emerge from the Cardinal blinking back the sunlight, holding two oranges and half a lime. Thea's awake by then, standing in the car park staring nonplused at the hand-painted sign in front of the roadhouse's fiberglass whale: *Please Keep Off The Whale.*

You slept? I ask her.

A bit.

You should eat something.

She looks doubtfully at my handfuls of citrus.

Something substantial, I tell her.

She's the kind of person who wants to hear the history of everything—what the chicken in her risotto was fed on, where the fabric of her shirt was made. I'm relieved when she just asks for a toasted sandwich.

We sit at one of the shaded picnic tables, unwrapping our sandwiches, washing them down with a warm bottle of beer I found under the driver's seat. The pale band of skin still shows on Thea's ring finger. She keeps her left hand splayed in direct sunlight, the faster to scorch the mark away.

Like a brand, she says, squinting at the ghost ring. Like

I'm one of those men, she says, one of those sad bullshitters you see drinking in the bars of chain hotels the whole world over. Hoping to pick up some exotic *concha* while my wife and my kids are on the other side of the world, getting dressed up to Skype me.

You don't have kids, I tell her. You don't even have a wife anymore, and she flicks a sandwich crust at me.

Look, she says, I'm not asking what your little side business is here.

I cram my mouth with the last corner of greasy ham-and-cheese and shake my head. Good, I'm not telling.

But if they search us at the border . . .

They won't find anything. There's nothing to find on this leg.

She looks back at the truck as though it might burst into flames. Shit, she says. Okay, I am asking.

I'm still not telling. Really, I promise. What does the west coast have that the east coast wants?

I don't know, she says. Giant Sandwiches? Why do you even need to make all this money?

Do you mean, Why do I need to make all this money for *myself*? Because most of us don't get it handed to us in a sparkly fucking envelope.

It wasn't like that, Thea says quietly.

For a while we're stranded there, silent, with the discarded takeaway wrappers, the gray wood of the railway-sleeper table carved up with decades of names, cocks and balls and cartoon hearts, until Thea rescues us both by reaching across for my wrist, tapping the place where a watch used to be.

That night I wake gasping for breath, the air in the tent blood-warm, near rancid. I gulp it down and the tent seems to breathe along with me, expanding and contracting, a dirty canvas lung. Swiping at the walls I finally find the fly, unzip the screen, and fall out onto the dirt. Twelve feet away, the Cardinal squats, grainy in the early dark. Loose-moleculed—I could put a hand right through it. Reach through the aluminum walls and shake Thea by her bony ankle. *You're still doing it, aren't you?*

A fish-belly blue is creeping in at the edge of the sky. I unfold a camping chair and sit at the little card table still crowded with sauce-encrusted plastic plates and burned-down candles, the syrupy dregs of a ten-dollar wine. What's left half-fills a mug and I sit there nursing it, staring out at the highway. Waiting for morning and the bone man but only one of them shows. Daylight burns off the bad dreams like fog but the roos and the dogs lie where they're scattered.

Past the border the coast leaps up to chomp at the desert for two hundred Ks of toothy scarp. Wrecks slide past the passenger window, inland side, and Thea lets them go without a word. On the stereo a Spanish audio guide repeats transactional phrases hypnotically: *I would like, I would like . . . I can't find my, I can't find my . . . Shoes. Coat. Wallet. Keys.* I mangle one word after the next while picturing the losing of all of these things, a room I have to keep walking back into. *I can't find my . . . Book. Phone. Dog. Daughter.* This pulls me away from the ache in my back and the cramp in my gut, away from the stuffy cab with its smell of roadhouse food and dirty clothes. *I would like, I would like* . . . until Thea snaps it off.

Fuck, you know what I would like?

It's a language, Thea. You can't be angry at a language.

Since when were you interested in learning Spanish? What's wrong with French or Italian?

I try to think of a joke, something to soften her face, but it's treacherous territory and too hot to tread it. I just drive. Then I speak up.

I thought you'd be away longer. I thought it would come in handy.

Right, she says, sorry, and the word seems as foreign, coming from her, as *zapato* or *escudo*.

A person probably can't be angry at a liqueur either, she says. But every time I get a whiff of Fernet-Branca I want to be sick.

Well. I reckon you're safe out here. Though I'd like to see the look you get, trying to order one.

A hand-painted sign pointing south promises three whales for five dollars. A decent unit price, concludes Thea. We pull off the highway, leave the truck and caravan crouching in the shade of retirement-funded fifth-wheelers, and follow the boardwalk out along the bluff. But there is only the one whale. At first we can't make sense of it, the sad pattern that goes:

Buoy. Whale and buoy. Buoy. Nothing. Buoy. Whale and buoy. Buoy. Nothing.

Tangled, we finally understand. The bright orange ball

bobbing up to the surface of the ocean, and the whale breaching a few seconds after. Then diving again, pulling the marker down with it.

Is there something we're supposed to do? Thea asks. Like some hotline we should call?

What could they do?

We stand there half an hour, letting the wind lift our clothes from our damp skin while the whale tows the buoy out to sea.

What's it like out there?

I don't know, I tell her, I've pretty much forgotten life as a whale.

On the rig, smart-arse.

Like living on a ship on stilts. In the galley of a ship on stilts.

Yeah, that's what I thought. I think I'd love that.

You'd hate it. There's nowhere to run.

But do they like you out there, those guys? Do they appreciate your cheffing?

My effing cheffing . . .

Those hi-vis guys do not say *effing*.

No, I say, they do not. And I don't know if you could call it *cheffing*, making vats of ham and scram for a hundred and twenty FIFOs. It's not exactly haute cuisine.

So come back to landlubbing, she says. Start a food truck or whatever it is you people do nowadays.

But I do like the money, I admit, because this is true. I like the helicopter rides. The correctional-orange overalls. The complete and total annihilation of anything resembling a body clock.

Thea gives me a sweet, sad smile. *One day*, I think. *One day I am going to . . .* but I can't imagine any further than my tongue circling her nipple, her navel. Her hands in my hair, guiding me down. I can't see how sex with Thea becomes a life with Thea. I turn my back on the ocean, grind the heels of my palms into my eyes till colors flood in.

Why don't you let me drive awhile, she says.

With the caravan?

It's not like I have to do a three-point turn with the thing, she says. Or, you know. Even a one-point turn. I'll go bats if I'm just sitting there, riding shotgun the whole way. I can take us as far as Ceduna, at least. I can do that far. You have a go at sleeping.

From here I only wake twice: the first time as Thea pulls over to the shoulder at dusk. She shirks out of her jeans, rolls her briefs down her legs, balls them up and stuffs them into the glove box. Then she goes out into the darkness to piss standing up, leaning back like a man. This might have seemed something like intimacy if I'd never watched her destroy a Datsun.

The second time I wake it's properly dark, desert dark. We're stopped again, in the middle of the highway. Thea is motionless behind the wheel, bare-legged, her briefs back on but her jeans still crumpled on the floor, tangled up around the clutch.

You're okay? I ask. Then I see him picked up in the high beams—a kid in a gray hoodie, standing still as a spotlit animal. Hood so low I can't make out his face, but one of his arms is raised over his head, a brick in his fist.

I don't know how long we sit there, the truck idling beneath us, Thea's bleak post-rock surging and dying away and surging again in sad orchestral waves until I reach across and turn it off. We wait for the kid to drop the brick and bolt, or to spring forward and launch it through the windscreen, but he never moves.

Wouldn't his arm be tired by now? murmurs Thea. Wouldn't it be asleep?

I don't know, I tell her.

Where'd he even find a brick out here anyway?

I shake my head; it doesn't matter. I make to crack the door and Thea says, Don't. Please just don't. So I wind down the window instead. Stick my head and shoulders out of it and scan the darkness beyond the highway, the black of the world that our headlights can't touch. He wouldn't be alone, not in this place—somewhere out there a gang of kids are crouched with sticks and knives. A jerry can of petrol. Dangerous boredom. I listen, straining to hear the inevitable ransacking of the Cardinal, but there's nothing yet. Just the white noise of insects, the song of the baked earth cooling.

I yell out, Hey! and the night takes my voice and throws it back at me, but the kid with the brick doesn't even flinch. I yell out, Hey, you little shit, put the fucking brick down. Nothing. I pull myself back into the car and wind the window up.

Forget it, I tell Thea. Some bullshit backwater prank. Just go on—he'll move all right. Or you want me to?

No, she says. I'm okay.

Thea lifts her foot from the brake, and the truck creeps forward, closing, inch by inch, the distance between us and the hooded kid.

You wanna give him reason to move, I tell her, and she puts her foot down and we jerk forward.

Then everything happens as in a movie we've already seen. We get close enough to see his face, the way it tightens. The intent to damage. We get close enough to see his skinny arm flex.

Then comes the sickening lurch as Thea brakes again. The symmetry of our flight from the Ranger, Thea still barelegged, white cotton briefs like an Elvis dream turned nightmare. She gets down on all fours to look under the bed and we meet that way, across those few feet of dreadful space, the heat of the day still there in the road beneath our bellies.

I am there, half under the truck, Thea's face showing me my own terror. And I am also somewhere far off. Somewhere high above us, a satellite's distance, where nothing that is happening or about to happen down in that scumbled expanse is of any consequence at all.

It's from that height that I'm whispering, Move. Move now. Please. Knowing that neither of us will hear.

What Passes for Fun

Somewhere close to the end of things, we drive past a pond and see that only its frozen surface remains, two inches thick and half an acre across, just levitating there. How is this possible? we ask ourselves, and we stop the car to look. The pond's surface has frozen around a stand of cattails, and that's what is propping it up now—all those thin, hollow stalks—as though it were the canopy of some modest structure, something we might assemble on a beach or in some other treeless place to keep the sun off the babies.

Everything beneath the ice has drained away, everything that was not solid. Where the cattails stop, so does that unlikely architecture; here is the edge of the frozen sheet, clean and deliberate as a cross-section, the fogged blue of sea glass. We can see where the cattails pass through the ice, spearing it, reaching on into the January sky and holding the pond surface up there triumphantly, three feet above the ground. Beyond the cattails, the surface lies in hard white pieces in the empty bed, shattered like an opaque mirror.

The babies want to crawl in under there and play, but we don't let them. A few broken stalks and the ice ceiling might collapse and crush them. But we understand the impulse. They have only recently learned to walk, to fling themselves clumsily between what they have and what they want. You and I have been upright for decades (not having gained much grace for all that) and still we'd like to walk out onto it, onto the lofted ice, to see if this implausibility can hold our weight. But we are superstitious. Because even though we can envisage the chain of events that might cause such a thing to happen—a blocked drain, a snap freeze, an unblocked drain, the surprising but not impossible strength of cattails—it is still magic. It is magic in the sense that there is no metaphor you can build out of it that will not undermine its magic. We stand at the roadside looking out at it for ten or fifteen minutes, holding tight to our daughters, who flap belligerently at the ends of our fingers like poorly trained kestrels. Then we get back into the car and drive to your sister's house, where the salmon is overdone and nothing extraordinary happens. Where we try with our rickety metaphors, and cannot even get them to judder across the table. We watch them fall over between the salt shaker and the cruet stand. Your sister grows tired of humoring us and begins clearing the dinner plates with their neat little piles of translucent bones.

What passes for fun with you two, she says. Christ Almighty.

While your sister is in the kitchen I swipe through the photographs, and find every one of them wanting, paling in comparison to the remembered pond. I hold the phone up for you to look.

This isn't quite it, is it?

No, you say, leaning across the table. That just looks like an ordinary frozen pond.

Several hours and many miles before the uplifted pond, I had prayed in a vague and wordless sort of way to whatever nameless thing we entreat when we do not believe in God. It's hypocritical, you've told me this. To still want signs. To scratch for evidence of predestination—something bigger than ourselves with its chin above our heads, its paws upon our shoulders. Something to tell us, Yes, go on, this is the way to go.

But at your sister's table we are still working with what we have. What we have is whatever hasn't drained away. I say this aloud. I am that dumb. I wind it up and I let it go, watch it teeter then topple over (salt shaker, cruet stand) before it gets to you. Sitting right there across from me, still hopeful. Still waiting for something you can trust your weight on.

Acknowledgments

Thank you to everyone at Catapult for spending another book with me. To the (probably) supernatural Jonathan Lee, Alicia Kroell, and the fabulous Wah-Ming Chang.

Thank you, Nicole Caputo and Jenny Carrow, for capturing the collective aura of these stories.

To Claudia Ballard, my ongoing gratitude for your faith. Thank you, Jessie Chasan-Taber.

Thank you to all at Black Inc. in Australia, especially to Julia Carlomagno and Chris Feik for their care and close attention, and to Marian Blythe for the moxie.

Thank you, Aviva Tuffield, for urging this collection into being, and for your encouragement over the years.

Thank you to the Wallace Stegner Program at Stanford, and to the Fiction Fellows of 2014, 2015, and 2016.

Thank you, Carmel and Ted Pittman, for sharing extraordinary places; Vanessa and Neil Boyack (sorry about the piano); Lisa Lang and Gerard Butera for milk bar nights. Thank you, Michelle de Kretser and Chris Andrews, for kindness, guidance, and vitamin C.

Thanks to Louise Glück, for the August sun.

Thank you, Yoann Gentric and Billy Exton, for the spider on the ceiling and French repairs. Thanks to Alice Bishop, Garnette Cadogan, and Wayne Macauley.

Thank you, Maxine Beneba Clarke. Thank you, Jennifer Mills. Thank you, Mireille Juchau.

Thank you, Derek Shapton, for not demanding a smile.
To Angela Meyer, for being a friend and a force.
To Patrick Pittman, for being a cardinal point through all these years, all these stories and the places they drew from.
To Jonny Diamond, for reaching across so much distance, again and again.

*

Several of the stories in this collection have appeared, in earlier versions, in the following publications: "Sinkers" in *The Monthly*, "Horse Latitudes" as "What Falls Away" in *Review of Australian Fiction*, "A Small Cleared Space" in *Overland*, "What Passes For Fun" in *The Canary Press* and *The Scofield*, "Glisk" in *Australian Book Review* (as the winner of the 2016 Elizabeth Jolley Short Story Prize), "Post-Structuralism for Beginners" in *Overland*, and "Anything Remarkable" in *Australian Book Review*.

*

I remain deeply grateful for the time, focus, and cultural exchange fostered by several organizations during the writing of this book: the BR Whiting Studio in Rome; the Yaddo Artists' Colony in Saratoga Springs, New York; and The Hermitage in Sarasota, Florida.

Thank you to the Copyright Agency's Cultural Fund for their generous support.